THIS BOOK BELONGS TO

_____

_____

_____

KING*f*ISHER

MILLY~MOLLY~MANDY STORIES

THE COMPLETE COLLECTION

KINGFISHER MODERN CLASSICS

ADVENTURES OF THE LITTLE WOODEN HORSE
URSULA MORAY WILLIAMS
ILLUSTRATED BY PAUL HOWARD

GOBBOLINO THE WITCH'S CAT
URSULA MORAY WILLIAMS
ILLUSTRATED BY PAUL HOWARD

MILLY-MOLLY-MANDY STORIES
JOYCE LANKESTER BRISLEY
ILLUSTRATED BY JOYCE LANKESTER BRISLEY

KINGFISHER CLASSICS

BLACK BEAUTY
ANNA SEWELL
ILLUSTRATED BY IAN ANDREW

TREASURE ISLAND
ROBERT LOUIS STEVENSON
ILLUSTRATED BY JOHN LAWRENCE

JOYCE LANKESTER BRISLEY

MILLY-MOLLY-MANDY STORIES

ILLUSTRATED BY
JOYCE LANKESTER BRISLEY

FOREWORD BY
SHIRLEY HUGHES

KING*f*ISHER

Publishers' Note:

The Publishers have used the first edition of *Milly-Molly-Mandy Stories*, published in Great Britain in 1928 by George G. Harrap & Co. Limited, for this publication. It is reproduced here complete and unabridged.

KINGFISHER
An imprint of Kingfisher Publications Plc
New Penderel House, 283-288 High Holborn, London WC1V 7HZ

First published by George G. Harrap & Co. Limited in 1928
This edition published by Kingfisher 2001
10 9 8 7 6 5 4 3 2 1
ITR/0601/THOM/MAR/1151NDWF(W)

These stories and most of the drawings first appeared in the Children's Page of *The Christian Science Monitor.*

Text and illustrations copyright © Joyce Lankester Brisley 1928
Foreword copyright © Shirley Hughes 2001
Author Note copyright © Kingfisher Publications Plc 2001
Cover illustration copyright © Clara Vulliamy 2001

A CIP catalogue record for this book is available from the British Library.

ISBN 0 7534 0593 8

Printed in India

It's good to be sitting still,
    And it's good to be running wild,
And it's good to be by yourself alone
    Or with another child.

And whether the child's grown up,
    Or whether the child is small,
So long as it really is a Child
    It doesn't matter at all.

                J. L. B.

The Nice White Cottage
with the Thatched Roof
(where Milly-Molly-
Mandy lives)

The Meadow
(where M-M-M and
Billy Blunt practised
racing)

The Barn
(where M-M-M
gave a party)

Brook

The
Moggs' Cottage
(where little-friend-
Susan lives)

Short cut to School
(only used in dry weather)

Woods

The Blackberry
Patch

(where M-M-M and
little-friend-Susan
did not go
blackberrying)

To Another Village

Map of the

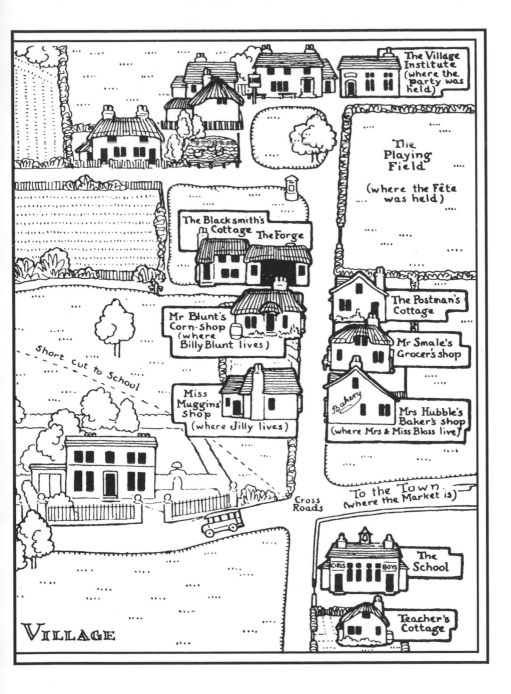

CONTENTS

FOREWORD

ONE DAY, about seventy-five years ago, a lady called Joyce Lankester Brisley sketched a picture of a family on the back of an envelope. It was a country family, standing in a row: Grandpa, Grandma, Father, Mother, Uncle, Aunty – and a lively little girl with bobbed hair wearing a striped dress. Joyce named her Milly-Molly-Mandy ("a long name, though she was so little") and the stories she went on to write and illustrate about her have that special something that makes children still want to read them, even in our own very different times.

The cosy, warm, "nice white cottage with a thatched roof" where Milly-Molly-Mandy lives seems a very real place, not a sugary-sweet make-believe one. And the ordinary doings of her life are full of small satisfactions and achievements: respect for animals and things as well as people, and some joyful celebrations.

I loved them from the start, from the first time I came across them when I was about the same age as Milly-Molly-Mandy herself. I read and reread them, over and over, tracing her comings and goings around the village with my finger on the important picture-map which appears at the front of this book: the short cut across the fields to school, the forge where the blacksmith hammers out iron horseshoes, the pond, the houses where her friends Billy Blunt, little-friend-Susan and Miss Muggins's Jilly live. There are no cars in the picture, just one bus driving past the Big House. There was very little traffic then, not even many bicycles. Children walked everywhere, very often on their own, ran messages for the grown-ups, went to play with their friends, and roamed about freely in the fields and woods much more than children do today. Nearly all the stories happen in or around the village. Sometimes Milly-Molly-Mandy drives into the nearby market town with Grandpa or Uncle in the "trap", drawn by Twinkletoes the pony. But outings like the time when she and the other village children take a bus and then a train for a day trip to the seaside don't happen very often, and that makes them all the more exciting.

Joyce Lankester Brisley is very good at giving you exact details of Milly-Molly-Mandy's home: the rush-seated wooden chairs, the dresser with its rows of plates and jugs, the rag rugs, the china ornaments on the fretwork corner shelf in the spare room. I felt I could move from room to room in that cottage and feel absolutely at home there. Now, when I am writing and illustrating my own "Alfie" stories, I remember how interesting it was to know so much about the background of a storybook character. I have a complete picture of Alfie's house and back garden, and his Grandma's house, in my head. I save up small details and store them away. I may not have put them all in yet, but I know I will need them one day.

Milly-Molly-Mandy and her family are always making and growing things. Very little is wasted or thrown away. All sorts of bits and pieces are carefully kept and come in useful again, like the scraps of ribbon and silk which Milly-Molly-Mandy collects to make a tea cosy for Mother, or Grandma's white silk scarf and Aunty's lace handkerchief which come out of the drawer to be made into a party frock for Milly-Molly-Mandy. There seem to be very few toys (except for the cotton-wool rabbit booby prize which she so much wanted) because she is mostly busy doing things outside with her friends and Toby the dog.

Food is very important, as it is in all the best stories: potato cakes, hot from the oven, blackberry jam and jelly, baked potatoes (called "lid potatoes", with a very exact description of how to make them), raspberry drops and aniseed balls from Miss Muggins's shop, and even the delicious clump of fresh mustard and cress which Milly-Molly-Mandy herself grows from seed and sells to Mrs Moggs for twopence.

Milly-Molly-Mandy plays her part in village life. She often has to take on quite serious tasks like going on an errand and remembering all the things she has to buy and how much each costs, minding the shop when Miss Muggins is called away, and working hard to help tidy and paint the house when Mother is away having a holiday. "My Muvver says we'd be like apple-trees which didn't grow apples if we didn't be useful" she tells Billy Blunt.

I suppose the world of Milly-Molly-Mandy is what we call an ideal one, where grown-ups are never cross or children naughty and quarrelsome. But when things in our own lives are sometimes difficult, reading these stories is like being wrapped up in a warm, reassuring blanket. Something we all need, now and again.

When I first read these stories, long ago, and later to my daughter Clara when she was a little girl, I never dreamed she would one day become an illustrator herself, and illustrate Milly-Molly-Mandy for the cover of this handsome new edition. Milly-Molly-Mandy has indeed become part of our lives and will, I hope, become part of yours too.

Shirley Hughes

London, 2001

1 MILLY-MOLLY-MANDY GOES ERRANDS

ONCE UPON A TIME there was a little girl.

She had a Father, and a Mother, and a Grandpa, and a Grandma, and an Uncle, and an Aunty; and they all lived together in a nice white cottage with a thatched roof.

This little girl had short hair, and short legs, and short frocks (pink-and-white-striped cotton in summer, and red serge in winter). But her name wasn't short at all. It was Millicent Margaret Amanda. But Father and Mother and Grandpa and Grandma and Uncle and Aunty couldn't very well call out "Millicent Margaret Amanda!" every time they wanted her, so they shortened it to "Milly-Molly-Mandy," which is quite easy to say.

Now everybody in the nice white cottage with the thatched roof had some particular job to do – even Milly-Molly-Mandy.

Father grew vegetables in the big garden by the cottage. Mother cooked the dinners and did the washing. Grandpa took the vegetables to market in his little pony-cart. Grandma knitted socks and mittens and nice warm woollies for them all. Uncle kept cows (to give them milk) and chickens (to give them eggs). Aunty sewed frocks and shirts for them, and did the sweeping and dusting.

And Milly-Molly-Mandy, what did she do?

Well, Milly-Molly-Mandy's legs were short, as I've told you, but they were very lively, just right for running errands. So Milly-Molly-Mandy was quite busy, fetching and carrying things, and taking messages.

One fine day Milly-Molly-Mandy was in the garden playing with Toby the dog, when Father poked his head out from the other side of a big row of beans, and said:

"Milly-Molly-Mandy, run down to Mr Moggs' cottage and ask for the trowel he borrowed from me!"

So Milly-Molly-Mandy said, "Yes, Farver!" and ran in to get her hat.

At the kitchen door was Mother, with a basket of eggs in her hand. And when she saw Milly-Molly-Mandy she said:

"Milly-Molly-Mandy, run down to Mrs

Moggs and give her these eggs. She's got visitors."

So Milly-Molly-Mandy said, "Yes, Muvver!" and took the basket. "Trowel for Farver, eggs for Muvver," she thought to herself.

Then Grandpa came up and said:

"Milly-Molly-Mandy, please get me a ball of string from Miss Muggins' shop – here's the penny."

So Milly-Molly-Mandy said, "Yes, Grandpa!" and took the penny, thinking to herself, "Trowel for Farver, eggs for Muvver, string for Grandpa."

As she passed through the kitchen Grandma, who was sitting in her armchair knitting, said:

"Milly-Molly-Mandy, will you get me a skein of red wool? Here's a sixpence."

So Milly-Molly-Mandy said, "Yes, Grandma!" and took the sixpence. "Trowel for Farver, eggs for Muvver, string for Grandpa, red wool for Grandma," she whispered over to herself.

As she went into the passage Uncle came striding up in a hurry.

"Oh, Milly-Molly-Mandy," said Uncle, "run like a good girl to Mr Blunt's shop, and tell him I'm waiting for the chicken-feed he promised to send!"

So Milly-Molly-Mandy said, "Yes, Uncle!" and thought to herself, "Trowel for Farver, eggs for Muvver, string for Grandpa, red wool for Grandma, chicken-feed for Uncle."

As she got her hat off the peg Aunty called from the parlour where she was dusting:

"Is that Milly-Molly-Mandy? Will you

get me a packet of needles, dear? Here's a penny!"

So Milly-Molly-Mandy said, "Yes, Aunty!" and took the penny, thinking to herself, "Trowel for Farver, eggs for Muvver, string for Grandpa, red wool for Grandma, chicken-feed for Uncle, needles for Aunty, and I do hope there won't be anything more!"

But there was nothing else, so Milly-Molly-Mandy started out down the path. When she came to the gate Toby the dog capered up, looking very excited at the thought of a walk. But Milly-Molly-Mandy eyed him solemnly, and said:

"Trowel for Farver, eggs for Muvver, string for Grandpa, red wool for Grandma, chicken-feed for Uncle, needles for Aunty. No, Toby, you mustn't come now, I've too much to think about. But I promise to take

GRANDPA · GRANDMA · FATHER · MOTHER · UNCLE · AUNTY · MILLY-MOLLY-MANDY.

you for a walk when I come back!"

So she left Toby on the other side of the gate, and set off down the road, with the basket and the pennies and the sixpence.

Presently she met a little friend, and the little friend said:

"Hello, Milly-Molly-Mandy! I've got a new see-saw! Do come on it with me!"

But Milly-Molly-Mandy looked at her solemnly and said:

"Trowel for Farver, eggs for Muvver, string for Grandpa, red wool for Grandma, chicken-feed for Uncle, needles for Aunty. No, Susan, I can't come now, I'm busy. But I'd like to come when I get back – after I've taken Toby for a walk."

So Milly-Molly-Mandy went on her way with the basket and the pennies and the sixpence.

Soon she came to the Moggs' cottage.

"Please, Mrs Moggs, can I have the trowel for Farver? And here are some eggs from Muvver!" she said.

Mrs Moggs was very much obliged indeed for the eggs, and fetched the trowel and a piece of seed-cake for Milly-Molly-Mandy's own self. And Milly-Molly-Mandy went on her way with the empty basket.

Next she came to Miss Muggins' little shop.

"Please, Miss Muggins, can I have a ball of string for Grandpa and a skein of red wool for Grandma?"

So Miss Muggins put the string and the wool into Milly-Molly-Mandy's basket, and took a penny and a sixpence in exchange. So that left Milly-Molly-Mandy with one penny. And Milly-Molly-Mandy couldn't remember what that penny was for.

"Sweeties, perhaps?" said Miss Muggins, glancing at the row of glass bottles on the shelf.

But Milly-Molly-Mandy shook her head.

"No," she said, "and it can't be chicken-feed for Uncle, because that would be more than a penny, only I haven't got to pay for it."

"It must be sweeties!" said Miss Muggins.

"No," said Milly-Molly-Mandy, "but I'll remember soon. Good morning, Miss Muggins!"

So Milly-Molly-Mandy went on to Mr Blunt's and gave him Uncle's message, and then she sat down on the doorstep and thought and thought what that penny could be for.

And she couldn't remember.

But she remembered one thing: "It's for Aunty," she thought, "and I love Aunty." And she thought for just a little while longer. Then suddenly she sprang up and went back to Miss Muggins' shop.

"I've remembered!" she said. "It's needles for Aunty!"

So Miss Muggins put the packet of needles into the basket, and took the penny, and Milly-Molly-Mandy set off for home.

"That's a good little messenger to remember all those things!" said Mother, when she got there. They were just going to begin dinner. "I thought you were only going with my eggs!"

"She went for my trowel!" said Father.

"And my string!" said Grandpa.

"And my wool!" said Grandma.

"And my chicken-feed!" said Uncle.

"And my needles!" said Aunty.

Then they all laughed; and Grandpa, feeling in his pocket, said:

"Well, here's another errand for you – go and get yourself some sweeties!"

So after dinner Toby had a nice walk and his mistress got her sweets. And then Milly-Molly-Mandy and little-friend-Susan had a lovely time on the see-saw, chatting and eating raspberry-drops, and feeling very happy and contented indeed.

2 MILLY-MOLLY-MANDY SPENDS A PENNY

ONCE UPON A TIME Milly-Molly-Mandy found a penny in the pocket of an old coat.

Milly-Molly-Mandy felt very rich indeed.

She thought of all the things she could buy with it, and there were so many that she did not know which to choose. (That is the worst of a penny.) So Milly-Molly-Mandy asked everybody with whom she lived, in the nice white cottage with the thatched roof, what they would do with it if they were her.

"Put it in the bank," said Grandpa promptly. He was making up accounts.

Milly-Molly-Mandy thought that a good idea.

"Buy a skein of rainbow wool and learn to knit," said Grandma, who was knitting by the kitchen door. Milly-Molly-Mandy thought that a good idea.

"Buy some seeds and grow mustard-and-cress," said Father, who was gardening. Milly-Molly-Mandy thought that quite a good idea.

"Buy a little patty-pan and make a cake in it," said Mother, who was cooking. Milly-Molly-Mandy thought that a very good idea.

"Save it up until you get three, and I'll let you buy a baby duckling with them," said Uncle, who was scooping out corn for his chickens. Milly-Molly-Mandy thought that an excellent idea.

"Get some sweets," said Aunty, who was

Milly-Molly-Mandy finds a penny

very busy sewing, and did not want to be interrupted. Milly-Molly-Mandy thought that a very pleasant idea.

Then she went to her own little corner of the garden for a "think", for she still could not make up her mind which of all those nice things to do. She thought and thought for a long time.

And then – what do you think she bought?

Some mustard-and-cress seeds, which

she planted in a shallow box of earth and stood in a nice warm place by the tool-shed.

She watered it every day, and shaded it if the sun were too hot; and at last the little seeds grew into a lovely clump of fresh green mustard-and-cress, that made you quite long for some bread-and-butter to eat it with.

When it was ready to cut Milly-Molly-Mandy went to Mrs Moggs, their neighbour down the road, who sometimes had summer visitors.

"Mrs Moggs," said Milly-Molly-Mandy, "if you should want some mustard-and-cress for your visitors' tea I have some to sell. It's very good, and quite cheap."

"Why, Milly-Molly-Mandy," said Mrs Moggs, "that's exactly what I am wanting! Is it ready for cutting now?"

So Milly-Molly-Mandy ran home and borrowed a pair of scissors and a little basket, and she snipped that lovely clump of fresh green mustard-and-cress (all but a tiny bit for her own tea) and carried it to Mrs Moggs.

And Mrs Moggs gave her twopence for it.

So Milly-Molly-Mandy had done one of the nice things and spent her penny, and now she had twopence!

Then Milly-Molly-Mandy took one of the pennies to the little village shop, and bought a skein of beautiful rainbow wool.

"Grandma," she said, when she got home, "please will you teach me to knit a kettle-holder?"

So Grandma found some knitting-needles and showed Milly-Molly-Mandy how to knit. And though it had to be undone several times at first, Milly-Molly-Mandy really did knit quite a nice kettle-holder, and there was just enough wool for it.

When she had put a loop in one corner to hang it up by she went to Mother, who was just putting the potatoes on to boil.

"Mother," said Milly-Molly-Mandy, "would you think this kettle-holder worth a penny?"

"Why, Milly-Molly-Mandy," said Mother, "that is exactly what I am wanting, for my old one is all worn out! But the penny only pays for the wool, so you are making me a present of all your trouble." And Mother gave Milly-Molly-Mandy a penny and a kiss, and Milly-Molly-Mandy felt well paid.

So Milly-Molly-Mandy had done another of the nice things, had spent her penny, and learnt to knit, and still she had her penny!

Then Milly-Molly-Mandy took her penny down to the little village shop and bought a shiny tin patty-pan. And next baking-day Mother let her make a little cake in the patty-pan and put it in the oven. And it was such a beautiful little cake, and so nicely browned, that it seemed almost too good to eat.

Milly-Molly-Mandy put it outside on the windowsill to cool.

Presently, along came a lady cyclist, and as it was a very hot day she stopped at the nice white cottage with the thatched roof, and asked Milly-Molly-Mandy's Mother if she could have a glass of milk. And while she was drinking it she saw the little cake on the windowsill, and the little cake looked so good that the lady cyclist felt hungry and asked if she could have that too.

Milly-Molly-Mandy's Mother looked at Milly-Molly-Mandy, and Milly-Molly-Mandy gave a little gulp, and said "Yes." And the lady cyclist ate up the little patty-cake. And she did enjoy it!

When she had gone Milly-Molly-Mandy's

Mother took up the pennies the lady cyclist had put on the table for the milk and the cake, and she gave one to Milly-Molly-Mandy because it was her cake.

So Milly-Molly-Mandy had done yet another of the nice things and spent her penny, but still she had her penny.

Then Milly-Molly-Mandy took her penny down to the little village shop and bought some sweets, lovely big aniseed-balls, that changed colour as you sucked them.

She would not eat one until she got home, and then gave one to Grandpa and one to Grandma and one to Father and one to Mother and one to Uncle and one to Aunty. And then she found there were six for herself, so she ate them, and they were very nice.

So Milly-Molly-Mandy had done another

of the nice things and spent her penny. But she still had one penny from the mustard-and-cress.

Then she went to Grandpa, and asked him please to put it in the bank for her.

And then she went to Uncle.

"Uncle," said Milly-Molly-Mandy, "I've done everything with my penny that everybody said, but you. And though I can't buy a little baby duckling yet, I've got a penny saved towards it, in the bank."

And it was not very long before Milly-Molly-Mandy had saved up to threepence; and then Uncle let her have a little yellow baby duckling all for her own.

3 MILLY-MOLLY-MANDY MEETS HER GREAT-AUNT

ONCE UPON A TIME, one fine evening, Milly-Molly-Mandy and her Father and Mother and Grandpa and Grandma and Uncle and Aunty were all sitting at supper (there was bread-and-butter and cheese for the grown-ups, and bread-and-milk for Milly-Molly-Mandy, and baked apples and cocoa for them all), when suddenly there came a loud *Bang-bang!* on the knocker.

"Run, Milly-Molly-Mandy," said Mother. "That sounds like the postman!"

So Milly-Molly-Mandy jumped down from her chair in a great hurry, and fetched the letter, which was for Mother. Then she climbed on her chair again, and everyone looked interested while Mother opened it.

It was from someone who called Milly-Molly-Mandy's Mother "Dear Polly," and was to ask if that someone might spend a few days with them, and it finished up, "Your affectionate Aunt Margaret."

Father and Mother and Grandpa and Grandma and Uncle and Aunty were quite pleased, and Milly-Molly-Mandy was pleased too, although she did not know who it was until Grandma said to her, "It is my

sister Margaret, your great-aunty, who is coming." Then Milly-Molly-Mandy was very interested indeed.

"Is she my great-aunty and your sister too?" she asked Grandma.

"Yes, and she's my sister-in-law," said Grandpa.

"And my aunty," said Mother.

"And my aunty-in-law," said Father.

"And my aunty-in-law too," said Aunty.

"And my aunty," said Uncle.

"Fancy!" said Milly-Molly-Mandy. "She's all that, and she's a great-aunty too! I would like to see her!"

The next day Milly-Molly-Mandy helped Mother make up the spare-room bed.

"I could wish the spare room were a little bigger," said Mother, and Milly-Molly-Mandy looked around gravely, and thought it really was rather small for a great-aunty. But she went and fetched some marigolds from her own little garden, and put them in a vase on the chest of drawers, for she knew there was lots of room for love, even if there was not much for great-aunties.

Then Milly-Molly-Mandy helped Father bring the big armchair out of the best parlour into the room where they always sat. Milly-Molly-Mandy was glad it was such a big chair – it really looked quite large enough even for a great-aunty.

Then Mother cooked some big fruit cakes and some little seedcakes and some sponge cakes and a whole lot of other things, and Milly-Molly-Mandy (who helped to clean up the cooking-bowls and spoons) supposed a great-aunty must take quite a lot of feeding.

As soon as ever the last bowl was scraped Milly-Molly-Mandy ran down the road to tell little-friend-Susan the news.

"That sounds like the postman!"

Little-friend-Susan was walking on the wall, but she jumped down as soon as she saw Milly-Molly-Mandy.

"Oh, Susan!" said Milly-Molly-Mandy, "you know my Aunty?"

"Yes," said little-friend-Susan.

"Well," said Milly-Molly-Mandy, "she's just a usual aunty, but I've got a great-aunty coming to stay with us!"

Little-friend-Susan, being a best friend, was just as interested as Milly-Molly-Mandy, and it was soon settled that next morning she should come and play in Milly-Molly-Mandy's garden, so that she might see Great-Aunty Margaret for herself.

Then Milly-Molly-Mandy ran back home to dinner.

After dinner Mother and Grandma and Aunty and Milly-Molly-Mandy hurried through the washing-up, and tidied the cottage, while Father put the pony in the trap. And then they changed their dresses, while Father drove to the station.

And then Milly-Molly-Mandy, in her clean frock, kept running to the gate to see if the pony-trap were in sight yet.

And at last it was – and Milly-Molly-Mandy was so excited that she raced into the cottage and jumped up and down, and then she ran out to the gate again, and opened it wide.

The pony trotted up to the gate and stopped, and Father got down first. And then he took down Great-Aunty Margaret's great basket. And then he helped down Great-Aunty Margaret her own self!

And what do you think Great-Aunty Margaret was like?

She was a little, little, white-haired lady, in a black bonnet and dress spotted with little mauve flowers, and she had a kind little face with pink cheeks.

Milly-Molly-Mandy was so surprised, it was all she could do to mind her manners and not stare.

Great-Aunty Margaret was soon seated in the great armchair, and instead of filling it, as Milly-Molly-Mandy had expected, why – there was heaps of room for Milly-Molly-Mandy there too! And instead of eating up all the big fruit cakes and the little seedcakes and the sponge cakes and other things, there was lots for everybody in the family, including Milly-Molly-Mandy.

And as for the spare room being too small, it looked almost big, because Great-Aunty Margaret was such a little lady.

When Great-Aunty Margaret saw the flowers on her chest of drawers she said gently:

"Why, Millicent Margaret Amanda, I believe that is your doing! Thank you, my dearie!"

"Oh, Great-Aunty Margaret!" said Milly-Molly-Mandy, reaching to kiss her again, "I do like you! Would you mind if I showed you to Susan this evening, instead of making her wait till tomorrow?"

4 MILLY-MOLLY-MANDY GOES BLACKBERRYING

ONCE UPON A TIME Milly-Molly-Mandy found some big ripe blackberries on her way home from school. There were six great beauties and one little hard one, so Milly-Molly-Mandy put the little hard one in her mouth and carried the others home on a leaf.

She gave one to Father, and Father said, "Ah! That makes me think the time for blackberry puddings has come!"

Then she gave one to Mother, and asked what it made her think of. And Mother said, "A whole row of pots of blackberry jam that I ought to have in my store-cupboard!"

Then she gave one to Grandpa, and Grandpa said it made him think "Blackberry tart!"

And Grandma said, "Blackberry jelly!"

And Uncle said, "Stewed blackberry-and-apple!"

And Aunty said, "A plate of blackberries with sugar and cream!"

"My!" thought Milly-Molly-Mandy, as she threw away the empty leaf, "I must get a big, big basket and go blackberrying the very next Saturday, so that there can be lots of puddings and jam and tarts and jelly and stewed blackberry-and-apple and fresh blackberries, for Farver and Muvver and Grandpa and Grandma and Uncle and Aunty – and me! I'll ask Susan to come too."

So the very next Saturday Milly-Molly-Mandy and little-friend-Susan set out with big baskets (to hold the blackberries) and hooked sticks (to pull the brambles nearer) and stout boots (to keep the prickles off) and old frocks (lest the thorns should catch). And they walked and they walked, till they came to a place where they knew there were always a lot of blackberries – at the proper time of year, of course.

But when they came to the place – oh, dear! – they saw a notice-board stuck up just inside a gap in the fence. And the notice-board said, as plain as anything:

TRESPASSERS
WILL BE
PROSECUTED

Milly-Molly-Mandy and little-friend-Susan set out

Milly-Molly-Mandy and little-friend-Susan knew that meant "You mustn't come here, because the owner doesn't want you, and it's his land."

Milly-Molly-Mandy and little-friend-Susan looked at each other very solemnly indeed. Then Milly-Molly-Mandy said, "I don't s'pose anyone would see if we went in."

And little-friend-Susan said, "I don't s'pose they'd miss any of the blackberries."

And Milly-Molly-Mandy said, "But it wouldn't be right."

And little-friend-Susan shook her head very firmly.

So they took up their baskets and sticks and moved away, trying not to feel hurt about it, although they had come a long way to that place.

They didn't know quite what to do with themselves after that, for there seemed to be no blackberries anywhere else, so they amused themselves by walking in a dry ditch close by the fence, shuffling along in the leaves with their stout little boots that were to have kept the prickles off.

And suddenly – what do you think they saw? A little ball of brown fur, just ahead of them among the grasses in the ditch.

"Is it a rabbit?" whispered little-friend-Susan. They crept closer.

"It is a rabbit!" whispered Milly-Molly-Mandy.

"Why doesn't it run away?" said little-friend-Susan, and she stroked it. The little ball of fur wriggled. Then Milly-Molly-Mandy stroked it, and it wriggled again.

Then Milly-Molly-Mandy exclaimed,

"I believe it's got its head stuck in a hole in the bank!"

And they looked, and that was just what had happened. Some earth had fallen down as bunny was burrowing, and it couldn't get its head out again.

So Milly-Molly-Mandy and little-friend-Susan carefully dug with their fingers, and loosened the earth round about, and as soon as bunny's head was free he shook his ears and stared at them.

Milly-Molly-Mandy and little-friend-Susan sat very still, and only smiled and nodded gently to show him he needn't be afraid, because they loved him.

And then little bunny turned his head and ran

skitter-scutter along the ditch and up the bank, into the wood and was gone.

"Oh!" said Milly-Molly-Mandy, "we always wanted a rabbit, and now we've got one, Susan!"

"Only we'd rather ours played in the fields with his brothers and sisters instead of stopping in a poky hutch," said little-friend-Susan.

"And if we'd gone trespassing we should never have come here and found him," said Milly-Molly-Mandy. "I'd much rather have a little rabbit than a whole lot of blackberries."

And when they got back to the nice white cottage with the thatched roof, where Milly-Molly-Mandy lived, Father and Mother and Grandpa and Grandma and Uncle and Aunty all said they would much rather have a little rabbit running about in the woods than all the finest blackberries in the world.

However, the next Saturday Milly-Molly-Mandy and little-friend-Susan came upon a splendid place for blackberrying, without any notice-board; and Milly-Molly-Mandy gathered such a big basketful that there was enough to make blackberry puddings and jam and tarts and jelly and stewed blackberry-and-apple and fresh blackberries for Father and Mother and Grandpa and Grandma and Uncle and Aunty – and Milly-Molly-Mandy too.

And all the time a little rabbit skipped about in the woods and thought what a lovely world it was.

(And that's a true story!)

5 MILLY-MOLLY-MANDY
   GOES TO A PARTY

ONCE UPON A TIME something very nice
happened in the village where Milly-Molly-
Mandy and her Father and Mother and
Grandpa and Grandma and Uncle and
Aunty lived. Some ladies clubbed together
to give a party to all the children in the
village, and of course Milly-Molly-Mandy
was invited.

Little-friend-Susan had an invitation too,
and Billy Blunt (whose father kept the corn-
shop where Milly-Molly-Mandy's Uncle got
his chicken-feed), and Jilly, the little niece
of Miss Muggins (who kept the shop where

Milly-Molly-Mandy's Grandma bought her knitting-wool), and lots of others whom Milly-Molly-Mandy knew.

It was exciting.

Milly-Molly-Mandy had not been to a real party for a long time, so she was very pleased and interested when Mother said, "Well, Milly-Molly-Mandy, you must have a proper new dress for a party like this. We must think what we can do."

So Mother and Grandma and Aunty thought together for a bit, and then Mother went to the big wardrobe and rummaged in her bottom drawer until she found a most beautiful white silk scarf, which she had worn when she was married to Father, and it was just wide enough to be made into a party frock for Milly-Molly-Mandy.

Then Grandma brought out of her best handkerchief box a most beautiful lace handkerchief, which would just cut into a little collar for the neck of the party frock.

And Aunty brought out of her small top drawer some most beautiful pink ribbon, all smelling of lavender – just enough to make into a sash for the party frock.

And then Mother and Aunty set to work to cut and stitch at the party frock, while Milly-Molly-Mandy jumped up and down and handed pins when they were wanted.

The next day Father came in with a paper parcel for Milly-Molly-Mandy bulging in his coat-pocket, and when Milly-Molly-Mandy unwrapped it she found the most beautiful little pair of red shoes inside!

And then Grandpa came in and held out his closed hand to Milly-Molly-Mandy, and when Milly-Molly-Mandy got his fingers open she found the most beautiful little coral necklace inside!

And then Uncle came in, and he said to Milly-Molly-Mandy, "What have I done with my handkerchief?" And he felt in all his pockets. "Oh, here it is!" And he pulled out the most beautiful little handkerchief with a pink border, which of course Milly-Molly-Mandy just knew was meant for her, and she wouldn't let Uncle wipe his nose on it, which he pretended he was going to do!

Milly-Molly-Mandy was so pleased she hugged everybody in turn – Father, Mother, Grandpa, Grandma, Uncle and Aunty.

At last the great day arrived, and little-friend-Susan, in her best spotted dress and

At last the great day arrived

silver bangle, called for Milly-Molly-Mandy, and they went together to the village institute, where the party was to be.

There was a lady outside who welcomed them in, and there were more ladies inside who helped them to take their things off. And everywhere looked so pretty, with garlands of coloured paper looped from the ceiling, and everybody in their best clothes.

Most of the boys and girls were looking at a row of toys on the mantelpiece, and a lady explained that they were all prizes, to be won by the children who got the most marks in the games they were going to have. There was a lovely fairy doll and a big teddy bear and a picture-book and all sorts of things.

And at the end of the row was a funny little white cotton-wool rabbit with a pointed paper hat on his head. And directly Milly-Molly-Mandy saw him she wanted him dreadfully badly, more than any of the other things.

Little-friend-Susan wanted the picture-book, and Miss Muggins' niece, Jilly, wanted the fairy doll. But the black, beady eyes of the little cotton-wool rabbit gazed so wistfully at Milly-Molly-Mandy that she determined to try ever so hard in all the games and see if she could win him.

Then the games began, and they were fun! They had a spoon-and-potato race, and musical chairs, and putting the tail on the donkey blindfold, and all sorts of guessing-games.

And then they had supper – bread-and-butter with coloured hundreds-and-thousands sprinkled on, and red jellies and yellow jellies, and cakes with icing and cakes with cherries, and lemonade in red glasses.

It was quite a proper party.

And at the end the names of prize-winners were called out, and the children had to go up and receive their prizes.

And what do you think Milly-Molly-Mandy got?

Why, she had tried so hard to win the little cotton-wool rabbit that she won first prize instead, and got the lovely fairy doll! And Miss Muggins' niece Jilly, who hadn't won any of the games, got the little cotton-wool rabbit with the sad, beady eyes – for do you know, the cotton-wool rabbit was only the booby prize, after all!

It was a lovely fairy doll, but Milly-Molly-Mandy was sure Miss Muggins' Jilly wasn't loving the booby rabbit as it ought to be loved, for its beady eyes did look so sad, and when she got near Miss Muggins' Jilly she stroked the booby rabbit, and Miss Muggins' Jilly stroked the fairy doll's hair.

Then Milly-Molly-Mandy said, "Do you love the fairy doll more than the booby rabbit?"

And Miss Muggins' Jilly said, "I should think so!"

So Milly-Molly-Mandy ran up to the lady who had given the prizes, and asked if she and Miss Muggins' Jilly might exchange prizes, and the lady said, "Yes, of course."

So Milly-Molly-Mandy and the booby rabbit went home together to the nice white cottage with the thatched roof, and Father and Mother and Grandpa and Grandma and Uncle and Aunty all liked the booby rabbit very much indeed.

And do you know, one day one of his little bead eyes dropped off, and when Mother had stuck it on again with a dab of glue, his eyes didn't look a bit sad any more, but almost as happy as Milly-Molly-Mandy's own!

6 MILLY-MOLLY-MANDY ENJOYS A VISIT

ONCE UPON A TIME Milly-Molly-Mandy was invited to go for a little visit to an old friend of Mother's who lived in a near-by town. Uncle was to take her in the pony-trap on Saturday morning on his way to market, and fetch her on Sunday evening, so that she should be ready for school next day. So Milly-Molly-Mandy would spend a whole night away from home, which was very exciting to think of. But just a day or two before she was to go, Mother received a letter from her friend to say she was so sorry, but she couldn't have Milly-Molly-

Mandy after all, as a married son and his wife had come unexpectedly to pay her a visit.

Milly-Molly-Mandy had to try very hard not to feel dreadfully disappointed, for she had never been away from home by herself before, and she had been looking forward to it so much.

"Never mind, Milly-Molly-Mandy," said Mother, when Saturday morning arrived and Milly-Molly-Mandy came down to breakfast looking rather solemn, "there are nice things happening all the time, if you keep your eyes open to see them."

Milly-Molly-Mandy said, "Yes, Muvver," in a small voice, as she took her seat, though it didn't seem just then as if anything could possibly happen as nice as going away to stay.

But while Father and Mother and

Grandpa and Grandma and Uncle and Aunty and Milly-Molly-Mandy were at breakfast Mrs Moggs, who was little-friend-Susan's mother, came round in a great hurry without a hat. And Mrs Moggs told them how some friends who had to go to the town on business, had offered her a seat in their gig. And as Mrs Moggs' mother lived there Mrs Moggs thought it was a nice opportunity to go and see her, only she didn't like leaving Susan alone all day, Mr Moggs being out at work.

So Milly-Molly-Mandy's mother said, "Let her come round here, Mrs Moggs. Milly-Molly-Mandy would like to have her. And I don't suppose you'll be back till late, so she'd better spend the night here too."

Milly-Molly-Mandy was pleased, and Mrs Moggs thanked them very much indeed, and they all wished Mrs Moggs a nice trip, and then Mrs Moggs ran back home to get ready.

"Where will Susan sleep? In the spare room?" asked Milly-Molly-Mandy, making haste to finish her breakfast.

"Yes," said Mother, "and you had better sleep there too, to keep her company."

Milly-Molly-Mandy was very much pleased at that, for she had never slept in the spare room – her cot-bed was in one corner of Father's and Mother's room.

"Why, Muvver!" she said, "I can't have a visit of my own, but I'll just be able to enjoy Susan's instead, shan't I? P'r'aps it'll be almost quite as nice!"

She helped to wash up the breakfast things, and to make the spare-room bed, and to dust.

And then she was just looking out of the window, thinking how nice it would be for Susan to wake up in the morning with a new view outside, when what did she see but little-friend-Susan herself, trudging along up the road with a basket on one arm and her coat on the other. So she ran down to the gate to welcome her in.

And though Milly-Molly-Mandy and little-friend-Susan met almost every day, and very often spent the whole day together, somehow it felt so different to think little-friend-Susan was going to stay the night with Milly-Molly-Mandy that they couldn't help giving an extra skip or two after they had kissed each other.

Milly-Molly-Mandy took her to see Mother, and then they went up to the spare room to unpack little-friend-Susan's basket.

They put her nightgown and brush and comb and toothbrush and slippers in their proper places, and decided which sides of the bed they were going to sleep – and they found each wanted the side that the other one didn't, which was nice – though of course Milly-Molly-Mandy would have given little-friend-Susan first choice, anyway.

Then Milly-Molly-Mandy showed little-friend-Susan round the room, and let her admire the fat silk pin-cushion on the dressing-table, and the hair-tidy that Aunty had painted, and the ornaments on the chest of drawers – the china dogs with the rough-feeling coats, and the little girl with the china lace skirt.

And while they were looking at the fretwork bracket which Father had made for Mother before they were married, Aunty came running up to say Uncle was just going to drive to market, and they might go with him if they were quick.

So they scrambled into their coats and hats, and Milly-Molly-Mandy ran to ask Mother in a whisper if she might take a penny from her money-box to spend in town. And soon they were sitting up close together beside Uncle in the high pony-trap, while the little brown pony (whose name was Twinkletoes) trotted briskly along the white road.

Little-friend-Susan hadn't been for many drives. Milly-Molly-Mandy often went, but she enjoyed this one much more than usual, because little-friend-Susan was so interested and pleased with everything.

Billy Blunt was whipping a top outside his father's corn-shop as they drove through the village. They waved to him, and he waved back. And a little farther on Miss Muggins' niece, Jilly, was wheeling her doll's pram along the pavement, and called out, "Hello, Milly-Molly-Mandy! Hello, Susan!"

And then they drove along a road through cornfields, where the little green blades of wheat were busy growing up to make big loaves of bread – which is why you must never interrupt them by walking in the corn, even if you see a poppy.

When they came to the town there were crowds of people everywhere, shouting

Unpacking little-friend-Susan's basket

about the things they had to sell. And Milly-Molly-Mandy and little-friend-Susan followed Uncle about the market-place, looking at all the stalls of fruit and sweets and books and fish and clothes and a hundred other things.

Milly-Molly-Mandy spent her penny on a big yellow sugar-stick for little-friend-Susan, who broke it carefully in two, and gave her half.

When Uncle had done his business he took them to have dinner at a place where all the tables had marble tops, which made such a sharp clatter unless you put your glass down very gently. There were crowds of people eating at other tables round about, and a lot of talking and clattering of cups and plates. It was very exciting. Little-friend-Susan was having a splendid holiday.

When they had finished Uncle paid the bill and led the way back to where Twinkletoes was waiting patiently, munching in his nosebag. And off they drove again, clippety-cloppety, with Uncle's parcels stowed under the seat.

And when they got near home it did seem queer for Milly-Molly-Mandy and little-friend-Susan to go straight past the Moggs' cottage and not have to stop and say goodbye to each other. They squeezed each other's hand all the rest of the way home to the nice white cottage with the thatched roof, because they felt so pleased.

When bedtime drew near they had their baths together, just as if they were sisters. And then Milly-Molly-Mandy in her red dressing-gown, and little-friend-Susan in Grandma's red shawl, sat in front of the fire on little stools (with Toby the dog on one side, and Topsy the cat on the other), while Mother made them each a lid-potato for their suppers.

First Mother took two well-baked potatoes out of the oven. Then she nearly cut the tops off them – but not quite. Then she scooped all the potato out of the skins and mashed it up with a little salt and a little pepper and a lot of butter. And then she pushed it back into the two potato-skins, and shut the tops like little lids.

Then Milly-Molly-Mandy and little-friend-Susan were given a mug of milk and a plate of bread-and-butter, and one of the nice warm lid-potatoes. And they opened the potato-lids and ate out of them with little spoons.

They did enjoy their suppers.

And when the last bit was gone Mother said, "Now, you two, I've set the candle in your room, and I'll be up to fetch it in ten minutes."

So Milly-Molly-Mandy and little-friend-Susan kissed goodnight to Father and Mother and Grandpa and Grandma and Uncle and Aunty, and stroked Toby the dog and Topsy the cat. And then they went upstairs to bed, hopping and skipping all the way, because they were so pleased they were going to sleep together in the spare room.

And next day, when Mrs Moggs came round to tell how she had enjoyed her trip, and to fetch Susan, Milly-Molly-Mandy said, "Thank you very much indeed, Mrs Moggs, for Susan's visit. I have enjoyed it!"

7 MILLY-MOLLY-MANDY GOES GARDENING

ONCE UPON A TIME, one Saturday morning, Milly-Molly-Mandy went down to the village. She had to go to Mr Blunt's corn-shop to order a list of things for Uncle – and would Mr Blunt please send them on Monday without fail?

Mr Blunt said, "Surely, surely! Tell your uncle he shall have them first thing in the morning."

And then Milly-Molly-Mandy, who loved the smell of the corn-shop, peeped into the great bins, and dug her hands down into the maize and bran and oats and let them sift through her fingers. And then she said goodbye and came out.

As she passed the Blunts' little garden at the side of the shop she saw Billy Blunt's back, bending down just the other side of the palings. It looked very busy.

Billy Blunt was a little bigger than Milly-Molly-Mandy, and she did not know him very well, but they always said "Hello!" when they met.

So Milly-Molly-Mandy peeped through the palings and said, "Hello, Billy!"

Billy Blunt looked round for a moment and said, "Hello!" And then he turned back to his work.

But he didn't say, "Hello, Milly-Molly-Mandy!" and he didn't smile. So Milly-Molly-Mandy stuck her toes in the fence and hung on and looked over the top.

"What's the matter?" Milly-Molly-Mandy asked

"What's the matter?" Milly-Molly-Mandy asked.

Billy Blunt looked round again. "Nothing's the matter," he said gloomily. "Only I've got to weed these old flower-beds right up to the house."

"I don't mind weeding," said Milly-Molly-Mandy.

"Huh! You try it here, and see how you like it!" said Billy Blunt. "The earth's as hard as nails, and the weeds have got roots pretty near a mile long."

Milly-Molly-Mandy wasn't quite sure whether he meant it as an invitation, but anyhow she accepted it as one, and pushed open the little white gate and came into the Blunts' garden.

It was a nice garden, smelling of wallflowers.

Billy Blunt said, "There's a garden fork." So Milly-Molly-Mandy took it up and started work on the other side of the flower-bed which bordered the little brick path up to the house. And they dug away together.

Presently Milly-Molly-Mandy said, "Doesn't the earth smell nice when you turn it up?"

And Billy Blunt said, "Does it? Yes, it does rather." And they went on weeding.

Presently Milly-Molly-Mandy, pulling tufts of grass out of the pansies, asked, "What do you do this for, if you don't like it?"

And Billy Blunt, tugging at a dandelion root, grunted and said, "Father says I ought to be making myself useful."

"That's our sort of fruit," said Milly-Molly-Mandy.

"My Muvver says we'd be like apple-trees which didn't grow apples if we didn't be useful."

"Huh!" said Billy Blunt. "Funny idea, us growing fruit! Never thought of it like that." And they went on weeding.

Presently Milly-Molly-Mandy asked, "Why're there all those little holes in the lawn?"

"Dad's been digging out dandelions," said Billy Blunt. "He wants to make the garden nice."

Then Milly-Molly-Mandy said, "There's lots of grass here, only it oughtn't to be.

We might plant it in the holes."

"Umm!" said Billy Blunt, "and then we'll be making the lawn look as tidy as the beds. Let's!"

So they dug, and they turned the earth, and they pulled out what didn't belong there. And all the weeds they threw into a heap to be burned, and all the tufts of grass they carefully planted in the lawn. And after a time the flower-beds began to look most beautifully neat, and you could see hardly any bald places on the lawn.

Presently Mr Blunt came out of the shop on to the pavement. He had a can of green paint and a brush in his hand, and he reached over the palings and set them down among the daisies on the lawn.

"Hello, Milly-Molly-Mandy!" said Mr Blunt. "Thought you'd gone home. Well, you two have been doing good work on those beds there. Billy, I'm going to paint the water butt and the handle of the roller some time. Perhaps you'd like to do it for me? You'll have to clean off the rust first with sandpaper."

Billy Blunt and Milly-Molly-Mandy looked quite eager.

Billy Blunt said, "Rather, Dad!" And Milly-Molly-Mandy looked with great interest at the green can and the garden roller. But she knew she ought to be starting back to dinner at the nice white cottage with the thatched roof, or Father and Mother and Grandpa and Grandma and Uncle and Aunty would be wondering what had become of her. So she handed her garden fork back to Billy Blunt and walked slowly to the gate.

But Billy Blunt said, "Couldn't you come again after dinner? I'll save you some of the painting."

So Milly-Molly-Mandy gave a little skip and said, "I'd like to, if Muvver doesn't want me."

So after dinner, when she had helped with the washing-up, Milly-Molly-Mandy ran hoppity-skip all the way down to the village again. And there in the Blunts' garden was Billy Blunt, busy rubbing the iron bands on the water butt with a sheet of sandpaper.

"Hello, Billy!" said Milly-Molly-Mandy.

"Hello, Milly-Molly-Mandy!" said Billy Blunt.

He looked very hot and dirty, but he smiled quite broadly. And then he said, "I've saved the garden roller for you to paint – it's all sandpapered ready."

Milly-Molly-Mandy thought that was nice of Billy Blunt, for the sandpapering was the nasty, dirty part of the work.

Billy Blunt got the lid off the can, and stirred up the beautiful green paint with a stick. Then all by himself he thought of fetching a piece of newspaper to pin over her frock to keep her clean. And then he went back to rubbing the water butt, while Milly-Molly-Mandy dipped the brush carefully into the lovely full can of green paint, and started work on the lawn roller.

The handle had a pattern in wriggly bits of iron, and it was great fun getting the paint into all the cracks. And you can't imagine how beautiful and new that roller looked when the paint was on it.

Billy Blunt had to keep leaving his water butt to see how it was going on, because the wriggly bits looked so nice when they were green, and he hadn't any wriggly bits on his water butt.

By the end of the afternoon you ought to have seen how nice the garden looked! The flower-beds were clean and trim, the lawn tidied up, the water butt stood glistening green by the side of the house, and the roller lay glistening green on the grass.

And when Mr Blunt came out and saw it all he was pleased!

He called Mrs Blunt, and Mrs Blunt was pleased too. She gave them each a banana, and they ate them sitting on one of the corn-bins in the shop.

And afterwards Billy Blunt buried Milly-Molly-Mandy in the corn, right up to the neck. And when he helped her out again she was all bits of corn, down her neck, and in her socks, and on her hair. But Milly-Molly-Mandy didn't mind a scrap. She liked it.

8 MILLY-MOLLY-MANDY MAKES A COSY

ONCE UPON A TIME Milly-Molly-Mandy went out visiting, in her best hat and new shoes and white cotton gloves. Milly-Molly-Mandy felt very proper indeed. She walked down the road, past the Moggs' cottage, past Mr Blunt's corn-shop, till she came to Miss Muggins' small shop. For Milly-Molly-Mandy was going to tea with Miss Muggins and her little niece, Jilly.

Miss Muggins' shop and the passage behind smelt so interesting – like calico and flannelette and brown paper, with faint whiffs of peppermint and raspberry-drops.

(For Miss Muggins sold a few sweets too, from bottles in a shelf in her window.)

But the little sitting-room at the back of the shop smelt mostly of warm buttered scones and sugary cakes, for the table was all laid ready, and Miss Muggins and Jilly were waiting for her. And over the teapot in front of Miss Muggins was a most beautiful cosy, all made of odd-shaped pieces of bright-coloured silks and velvets, with loops of coloured cord on top. Milly-Molly-Mandy did like it!

After Milly-Molly-Mandy had eaten two buttered scones she couldn't help saying, "Isn't that a beautiful cosy!"

And Jilly said, "Aunty made it!"

Milly-Molly-Mandy thought how nice it would be to have such a beautiful cosy on the table at home.

She couldn't help saying, "Isn't that a beautiful cosy!"

When she had eaten a pink sugary cake she said, "Wasn't that cosy very difficult to make?"

And Miss Muggins (who had just come back from serving a lady with a card of linen buttons and some black elastic) said, "Oh, no, it was quite easy! You ought to get your aunty to teach you feather-stitching, Milly-Molly-Mandy, so that you could make one!"

Milly-Molly-Mandy thought how nice it would be to make Mother such a beautiful cosy, but she didn't know how she could get the stuffs.

After the meal she played with Jilly and her doll's house, and when it was time to go Miss Muggins came out of the shop with a small piece of bright red satin, to start Milly-Molly-Mandy making a cosy. Milly-Molly-Mandy was pleased!

Then she thanked Miss Muggins very much for having her, and ran back home to the nice white cottage with the thatched roof.

She hid the red satin in her doll's cradle, and wondered a great deal how she could get enough pieces of stuff to make a cosy.

And then, one morning, Mother turned out of her piece-bag some scraps of green ribbon, and said Milly-Molly-Mandy might have them. Milly-Molly-Mandy *was* pleased!

But as she didn't like the thought of Mother giving anything for her own secret present she looked round for something she could do in exchange for it. And she saw, behind the kitchen door, a muddy pair of Mother's shoes waiting to be cleaned. So Milly-Molly-Mandy quietly got out the boot-box and cleaned them.

So now Milly-Molly-Mandy had some red pieces and some green pieces.

And then, one afternoon, Father gave her a penny to buy some sweets. And Milly-Molly-Mandy said, "Would you mind, Farver, if I bought something else instead, for a great secret?"

And Father didn't mind, so Milly-Molly-Mandy went to Miss Muggins' shop and bought a skein of black silk to do the feather-stitching with.

So now Milly-Molly-Mandy had some red pieces and some green pieces and a skein of black silk.

And then, one day, Grandma altered her best dress, which was of velvet, and the bit she cut off she gave to Milly-Molly-Mandy to play with.

So now Milly-Molly-Mandy had some

red pieces and some green pieces and a skein of black silk and some black pieces.

And then, one morning, Grandpa let her come with him in the pony-trap to the town. And while they were there he looked in the shop windows and asked Milly-Molly-Mandy what she would like for a little present. And Milly-Molly-Mandy said, "Oh, Grandpa, could I have some coloured cord for a great secret?" So Grandpa bought her some coloured cord without asking any questions.

So now Milly-Molly-Mandy had some red pieces and some green pieces and a skein of black silk and some black pieces and some coloured cord.

And then, one afternoon, Aunty was retrimming a hat, and when she took off the old lavender ribbon it had on it she said

Milly-Molly-Mandy could have it. And Milly-Molly-Mandy found some parts of it were quite good.

So now Milly-Molly-Mandy had some red pieces and some green pieces and a skein of black silk and some black pieces and some coloured cord and some lavender pieces.

And then, one day, Uncle was turning over the neckties in his drawer, and there was one blue one with yellow spots which Uncle didn't like, and he threw it to Milly-Molly-Mandy, saying, "Here, Milly-Molly-Mandy, this'll do for a doll's sash, or something."

So now Milly-Molly-Mandy had some red pieces and some green pieces and a skein of black silk and some black pieces and some coloured cord and some lavender pieces and some blue pieces with yellow spots.

And Milly-Molly-Mandy thought she really had enough now to begin the cosy!

She went to Aunty and asked if she would kindly teach her to do feather-stitching for a great secret. So Aunty showed her how to cut up the pieces and feather-stitch them together.

And then, for weeks, Milly-Molly-Mandy spent nearly all her spare time in the attic or in the barn, sewing and sewing, and never showed anyone but Aunty what she was doing.

One evening Father said, "Whatever is Milly-Molly-Mandy up to these days?"

And Mother said, "I can't think."

And Grandpa said, "I haven't seen her properly for days."

And Grandma said, "I think she's got some kind of secret on."

And Uncle said, "I shouldn't be surprised."

But Aunty said nothing at all, and only put the tablecloth straight.

And then, just when Mother had finished laying the supper, Milly-Molly-Mandy came in with a very pink face and her hands behind her back.

Mother went to the oven to bring out a plate of hot potato-cakes. And when she turned round again, there, at her end of the table, was the most beautiful patchwork cosy keeping the cocoa-jug hot!

"Milly-Molly-Mandy!" said Mother.

She hurried to her place, while Milly-Molly-Mandy

jumped up and down, and Father and Grandpa and Grandma and Uncle and Aunty all looked on admiringly.

"Oh, Milly-Molly-Mandy!" said Mother, "what – a – *beautiful* – cosy!"

And Mother was so pleased, and Milly-Molly-Mandy was so glad she was pleased, that they just had to hug and kiss each other very hard indeed.

And the potato-cakes got almost cold, but the cocoa was just as hot as hot!

9 MILLY-MOLLY-MANDY KEEPS SHOP

ONCE UPON A TIME Milly-Molly-Mandy was walking home from school with some little friends – Billy Blunt, Miss Muggins' niece Jilly, and, of course, little-friend-Susan. And they were all talking about what they would like to do when they were big.

Billy Blunt said he would have a motor-bus and drive people to the station and pull their boxes about. Miss Muggins' Jilly said she would curl her hair and be a lady who acts for the pictures. Little-friend-Susan wanted to be a nurse with long white streamers, and push a pram with two babies in it.

Milly-Molly-Mandy wanted a shop like Miss Muggins, where she could sell sweets, and cut pretty coloured stuff for people's dresses with a big pair of scissors. And, "Oh, dear!" said Milly-Molly-Mandy, "I wish we didn't have to wait till we had growed up!"

Then they came to Miss Muggins' shop, and Jilly said "Goodbye," and went in.

And then they came to Mr Blunt's corn-shop which was only a few steps farther on, and Billy Blunt said "Goodbye," and went in.

And then Milly-Molly-Mandy and little-friend-Susan, with their arms round each other, walked up the white road with the fields each side till they came to the Moggs' cottage, and little-friend-Susan said, "Goodbye," and went in.

And Milly-Molly-Mandy went hoppity-skipping on alone till she came to the nice white cottage with the thatched roof, where Mother was at the gate to meet her.

Next day was Saturday, and Milly-Molly-Mandy went down to the village on an errand for Mother. And when she had done it she saw Miss Muggins standing at her shop door, looking rather worried.

And when Miss Muggins saw Milly-Molly-Mandy she said, "Oh, Milly-Molly-Mandy, would you mind running to ask Mrs Jakes if she could come and mind my shop for an hour? Tell her I've got to go to see someone on very important business, and I don't know what to do, and Jilly's gone picnicking."

So Milly-Molly-Mandy ran to ask Mrs Jakes. But Mrs Jakes said, "Tell Miss Muggins I'm very sorry, but I've just got the cakes in the oven, and I can't leave them."

So Milly-Molly-Mandy ran back and told Miss Muggins, and Miss Muggins said, "I wonder if Mrs Blunt would come."

So Milly-Molly-Mandy ran to ask Mrs Blunt. But Mrs Blunt said, "I'm sorry, but I'm simply up to my eyes in house-cleaning, and I can't leave just now."

So Milly-Molly-Mandy ran back and told Miss Muggins, and Miss Muggins said she didn't know of anyone else she could ask.

Then Milly-Molly-Mandy said, "Oh, Miss Muggins, couldn't I look after the shop for you? I'll tell people you'll be back in an hour, and if they only want a sugar-stick or something I could give it them – I know how much it is!"

Miss Muggins looked at Milly-Molly-Mandy, and then she said, "Well, you aren't very big, but I know you're careful, Milly-Molly-Mandy."

So she gave her lots of instructions about asking people if they would come back in an hour, and not selling things unless she was quite sure of the price, and so on. And then Miss Muggins put on her hat and feather boa and hurried off.

And Milly-Molly-Mandy was left alone in charge of the shop!

Milly-Molly-Mandy felt very solemn and careful indeed. She dusted the counter with a duster which she saw hanging on a nail; and then she peeped into the window at all the handkerchiefs and socks and bottles of sweets – and she could see Mrs Hubble arranging the loaves and cakes in her shop window opposite, and Mr Smale (who had the grocer's shop with a little counter at the back where you posted parcels and bought stamps and letter-paper) standing at his door enjoying the sunshine. And Milly-Molly-Mandy felt so pleased that she had a shop as well as they.

And then, suddenly, the door-handle rattled, and the little bell over the door jangle-jangled up and down, and who should come in but little-friend-Susan! And how little-friend-Susan did stare when she saw Milly-Molly-Mandy behind the counter!

"Miss Muggins has gone out on 'portant business, but she'll be back in an hour. What do you want?" said Milly-Molly-Mandy.

"A packet of safety-pins for Mother. What are you doing here?" said little-friend-Susan.

"I'm looking after the shop," said Milly-Molly-Mandy. "And I know where the safety-pins are, because I had to buy some yesterday."

So Milly-Molly-Mandy wrapped up the safety-pins in a piece of thin brown paper, and twisted the end just as Miss Muggins did. And she handed the packet to little-friend-Susan, and little-friend-Susan handed her a penny.

And then little-friend-Susan wanted to stay and play "shops" with Milly-Molly-Mandy.

But Milly-Molly-Mandy shook her head solemnly and said, "No, this isn't play: it's business. I've got to be very, very careful. You'd better go, Susan."

And just then the bell jangled again, and a lady came in, so little-friend-Susan went out. (She peered through the window for a time to see how Milly-Molly-Mandy got on, but Milly-Molly-Mandy wouldn't look at her.)

The lady was Miss Bloss, who lived opposite, over the baker's shop, with Mrs Bloss. She wanted a quarter of a yard of pink flannelette, because she was making a wrapper for her mother, and she hadn't bought quite enough for the collar. She said she didn't like to waste a whole hour till Miss Muggins returned.

Milly-Molly-Mandy stood on one leg and wondered what to do, and Miss Bloss tapped with one finger and wondered what to do.

And then Miss Bloss said, "That's the roll my flannelette came off. I'm quite sure Miss Muggins wouldn't mind my taking some."

So between them they measured off the pink flannelette, and Milly-Molly-Mandy fetched Miss Muggins' big scissors, and Miss Bloss made a crease exactly where the quarter-yard came; and Milly-Molly-Mandy breathed very hard and cut slowly and carefully right along the crease to the end.

And then she wrapped the piece up and gave it to Miss Bloss, and Miss Bloss handed her half a crown, saying, "Ask Miss Muggins to send me the change when she gets back."

And then Miss Bloss went out.

And then for a time nobody came in, and Milly-Molly-Mandy amused herself by trying to find the rolls of stuff that different people's dresses had come off. There was her own pink-and-white-striped cotton (looking so lovely and new) and Mother's blue checked apron stuff and Mrs Jakes' Sunday gown . . .

Then rattle went the handle and jangle went the bell, and who should come in but Billy Blunt!

"I'm Miss Muggins," said Milly-Molly-Mandy. "What do you want to buy?"

"Where's Miss Muggins?" said Billy Blunt.

So Milly-Molly-Mandy had to explain again. And then Billy Blunt said he had wanted a pennyworth of aniseed-balls.

So Milly-Molly-Mandy stood on a box and reached down the glass jar from the shelf. They were twelve a penny she knew, for she had often bought them. So she counted them out, and then Billy Blunt counted them.

And Billy Blunt said, "You've got one too many here."

So Milly-Molly-Mandy counted again, and she found one too many too. So they dropped one back in the jar, and Milly-Molly-Mandy put the others into a little bag and swung it over by the corners, just as Miss Muggins did, and gave it to Billy Blunt. And Billy Blunt gave her his penny.

And then Billy Blunt grinned, and said, "Good morning, ma'am."

"I'm Miss Muggins. What do you want to buy?"

And Milly-Molly-Mandy said, "Good morning, sir," and Billy Blunt went out.

After that an hour began to seem rather a long time, with the sun shining so outside. But at last the little bell gave a lively jangle again, and Miss Muggins had returned!

And though Milly-Molly-Mandy had enjoyed herself very much, she thought perhaps, after all, she would rather wait until she was grown up before she kept a shop for herself.

10 MILLY-MOLLY-MANDY GIVES A PARTY

ONCE UPON A TIME Milly-Molly-Mandy had a plan. And when she had thought over the plan for a while she went to look in her money-box. And in the money-box were four pennies and a ha'penny, which Milly-Molly-Mandy did not think would be enough for her plan. So Milly-Molly-Mandy went off to talk it over with little-friend-Susan down the road.

"Susan," said Milly-Molly-Mandy, "I've got a plan (only it's a great secret). I want to give a party in our barn to Farver and Muvver and Grandpa and Grandma and

Uncle and Aunty. And I want to buy refreshments. And you and I will be waitresses. And if there's anything over we can eat it up afterwards."

Little-friend-Susan thought it a very good plan indeed.

"Will we wear caps?" she asked.

"Yes," said Milly-Molly-Mandy, "and aprons. Only I haven't got enough money for the refreshments, so I don't think there'll be any over. We must think."

So Milly-Molly-Mandy and little-friend-Susan sat down and thought hard.

"We must work and earn some," said Milly-Molly-Mandy.

"But how?" said little-friend-Susan.

"We might sell something," said Milly-Molly-Mandy.

"But what?" said little-friend-Susan.

So they had to think some more.

Presently Milly-Molly-Mandy said, "I've got pansies and marigolds in my garden."

And little-friend-Susan said, "I've got nasturtiums in mine."

"We could run errands for people," said Milly-Molly-Mandy.

"And clean brass," said little-friend-Susan.

That was a lovely idea, so Milly-Molly-Mandy fetched a pencil and paper and wrote out very carefully:

Millicent Margaret Amanda & Susan & Co. have bunches of flowers for sale and clean brass very cheap (we do not spill the polish) and run errands very cheap.

"What's 'and Co.'?" said little-friend-Susan.

"It's just business," said Milly-Molly-Mandy, "but perhaps we might ask Billy Blunt to be it. And he could be a waiter."

Then they hung the notice on the front gate, and waited just the other side of the hedge.

Several people passed, but nobody seemed to want anything. Then at last a motor-car came along with a lady and gentleman in it; and when they saw the nice white cottage with the thatched roof they stopped at the gate to ask if they could get some cream there.

Milly-Molly-Mandy said, "I'll go and ask Muvver," and took the little pot they held out. And when she came back with it full of cream the lady and gentleman had read the notice and were asking little-friend-Susan questions. As the lady paid for the cream she said they must certainly have some flowers. So they each bought a bunch. And then the gentleman said the round brass thing in front of his car needed cleaning very badly – could the firm do it straight away?

So Milly-Molly-Mandy said, "Yes, sir," and raced back to the cottage to give Mother the cream-money and to borrow the brass-polishing box. And then she cleaned the round brass thing in front of the car with one piece of cloth and little-friend-Susan rubbed it bright with another piece of cloth, and the lady and gentleman looked on and seemed very satisfied.

Then the gentleman asked, "How much?" and paid them twopence for the flowers and a penny for the polishing. Milly-Molly-Mandy wanted to do some more polishing for the money, but the gentleman said they couldn't stop. And then they said goodbye and went off, and the lady turned and waved, and Milly-Molly-Mandy and little-friend-Susan waved back until they were gone.

Milly-Molly-Mandy and little-friend-Susan felt very happy and pleased.

And now they had sevenpence-ha'penny for the refreshments. Father and Mother and Grandpa and Grandma and Uncle and Aunty and Mrs Moggs, little-friend-Susan's mother, made seven.

Then who should look over the hedge but Mr Jakes, the Postman, on his way home from collecting letters from the letterboxes. He had seen the notice on the gate.

"What's this? You trying to make a fortune?" said the Postman.

"Yes," said Milly-Molly-Mandy, "we've earned threepence!"

"My! And what do you plan to do with it?" said the Postman.

"We've got a secret!" said Milly-Molly-Mandy, with a little skip.

"Ah!" said the Postman, "I guess it's a nice one, too!"

"Milly-Molly-Mandy looked at little-friend-Susan, and then she looked at the Postman. He was a nice Postman. "You won't tell if we tell you?" she asked.

"Try me!" said the Postman promptly. So Milly-Molly-Mandy told him they were planning to give a party to Father and Mother and Grandpa and Grandma and Uncle and Aunty and Mrs Moggs.

"They're in luck, they are!" said the Postman. "Nobody asks me to parties."

Milly-Molly-Mandy looked at little-friend-Susan again, and then she looked at the Postman. He was a very nice Postman. Then she said, "Supposing you were invited, would you come?"

"You try me!" said the Postman promptly again. And then he hitched up his letter-bag and went on.

"Farver and Muvver and Grandpa and Grandma and Uncle and Aunty and Mrs Moggs and the Postman. We've got to earn some more," said Milly-Molly-Mandy. "Let's go down to the village and ask Billy Blunt to be 'and Co.', and p'r'aps he'll have an idea."

Billy Blunt was in the road outside the corn-shop, mending the handles of his box on wheels. He had made it nearly all himself, and it was a very nice one, painted green like the water butt and the lawn roller. He thought "and Co." was rather a funny name, but said he would be it all right, and offered to make them a box with a slit in it, where they could keep their earnings. And he put in four farthings out of his collection. (Billy Blunt was collecting farthings – he had nineteen in an empty birdseed bag.)

So now they had eightpence-ha'penny for the refreshments.

On Monday morning, on their way home to dinner, Milly-Molly-Mandy and little-friend-Susan passed Mrs Jakes, the Postman's wife, at her door, getting a breath of fresh air before dishing up her dinner. And Mrs Jakes said, "Good morning! How's the firm of Millicent Margaret Amanda, Susan, and Co. getting on?"

Milly-Molly-Mandy said, "Very well, thank you!"

"My husband's told me about your brass-cleaning," said Mrs Jakes. "I've got a whole mantelshelf full that wants doing!"

Milly-Molly-Mandy and little-friend-Susan were very pleased, and arranged to come in directly school was over in the afternoon and clean it.

And they cleaned a mug and three candlesticks and two lamps – one big and one little – and a tray and a warming-pan, and they didn't spill or waste any of the polish. Mrs Jakes seemed very satisfied, and gave them each a penny and a piece of cake.

So now they had tenpence-ha'penny for refreshments.

But when they got outside Milly-Molly-Mandy said, "Farver and Muvver and Grandpa and Grandma and Uncle and Aunty and Mrs Moggs and the Postman and Mrs Postman – I wonder if we've earned enough, Susan?"

As they turned home they passed the forge, and of course they had to stop a moment at the doorway, as usual, to watch the fire roaring, and Mr Rudge the Blacksmith banging with his hammer on the anvil.

Little-friend-Susan was just a bit nervous of the Blacksmith – he was so big, and his face was so dirty it made his teeth look very white and his eyes very twinkly when he smiled at them. But Milly-Molly-Mandy knew he was nice and clean under the dirt, which he couldn't help while he worked. So she smiled back.

And the Blacksmith said, "Hello!"

And Milly-Molly-Mandy said, "Hello!"

Then the Blacksmith beckoned with his finger and said, "Come here!"

Milly-Molly-Mandy gave a little jump, and little-friend-Susan pulled at her hand, but Milly-Molly-Mandy knew he was really just a nice man under the dirt, so she went up to him.

And the Blacksmith said, "Look what I've got here!" And he showed them a tiny little horseshoe, just like a proper one, only smaller, which he had made for them to keep. Milly-Molly-Mandy and little-friend-Susan were pleased!

Milly-Molly-Mandy thanked him very

much. And then she looked at the Blacksmith and said, "If you were invited to a party, would you come?"

And the Blacksmith looked at Milly-Molly-Mandy with twinkly eyes and said he'd come quite fast – so long as it wasn't before five o'clock on Saturday, when he was playing cricket with his team in the meadow.

When they got outside again Milly-Molly-Mandy said, "Farver and Muvver and Grandpa and Grandma and Uncle and Aunty and Mrs Moggs and the Postman and Mrs Postman and the Blacksmith. We'll ask them for half-past five, and we ought to earn some more money, Susan!"

Just then they met Billy Blunt coming along, pulling his box on wheels with a bundle in it. And Billy Blunt grinned and said, "I'm fetching Mrs Bloss's washing, for the firm!" Milly-Molly-Mandy and little-friend-Susan were pleased!

When Saturday morning came all the invitations had been given out, and the firm of Millicent Margaret Amanda, Susan and Co. were very busy putting things tidy in the barn, and covering up things which couldn't be moved with lots of green branches which Grandpa was trimming from the hedges.

And when half-past five came Milly-Molly-Mandy and little-friend-Susan, with clean hands and paper caps and aprons, waited by the barn door to welcome the guests. And each gentleman received a marigold buttonhole, and each lady a pansy.

Everybody arrived in good time, except the Blacksmith, who was just a bit late – he looked so clean and pink in his white cricket flannels, Milly-Molly-Mandy hardly knew him – and Billy Blunt. But Billy Blunt came lugging a gramophone and two records which he had borrowed from a bigger boy at school. (He never told, but he had given the boy all the rest of his collection of farthings – fifteen of them, which makes threepence-three-farthings – in exchange.)

Then Billy Blunt, who didn't want to dance, looked after the gramophone, while Father and Mother and Grandpa and Grandma and Uncle and Aunty and Mrs Moggs and the Postman and Mrs Postman and the Blacksmith and Milly-Molly-Mandy and little-friend-Susan danced together in the old barn till the dust flew. And Milly-Molly-Mandy danced a lot with the Blacksmith as well as with everybody else, and so did little-friend-Susan.

They did enjoy themselves!

And then there were refreshments — raspberry-drops and aniseed-balls on saucers trimmed with little flowers; and late blackberries on leaf plates; and sherbet drinks, which Billy Blunt prepared while Milly-Molly-Mandy and little-friend-Susan stood by to tell people just the very moment to drink, when it was fizzing properly. (It was exciting!) And a jelly which Milly-Molly-Mandy and little-friend-Susan had made themselves from a packet, only it had to be eaten rather like soup, as it wouldn't stand up properly.

But Father and Mother and Grandpa and Grandma and Uncle and Aunty and Mrs Moggs and the Postman and Mrs Postman and the Blacksmith all said they had never enjoyed a jelly so much. And the Blacksmith, in a big voice, proposed a vote of thanks

And then there were refreshments

to the firm for the delightful party and refreshments, and everybody else said "Hear! Hear!" and clapped. And Milly-Molly-Mandy and little-friend-Susan joined in the clapping too, which wasn't quite proper, but they were so happy they couldn't help it!

And then all the guests went home.

And when the firm came to clear up the refreshments they found there was only one aniseed-ball left. But placed among the empty saucers and glasses on the bench were a small basket of pears and a bag of mixed sweets with a ticket "For the Waiter and Waitresses" on it!

11 MILLY-MOLLY-MANDY GOES VISITING

ONCE UPON A TIME Milly-Molly-Mandy had a letter. It was from Mrs Hooker, who had been a friend of Mother's ever since she was a little girl. And it said how sorry Mrs Hooker was to have put Milly-Molly-Mandy off last time she had invited her – that time Milly-Molly-Mandy had enjoyed little-friend-Susan's visit instead of her own. But now Mrs Hooker's son and his wife had gone abroad to live, and Mrs Hooker would be very pleased if Mother would let Milly-Molly-Mandy come and spend a weekend with her, as promised.

Milly-Molly-Mandy was very pleased, and Father and Mother and Grandpa and Grandma and Uncle and Aunty were very pleased for her. They talked of Milly-Molly-Mandy going away nearly all suppertime, and Aunty promised to put a new ribbon round her best hat, and Mother said she must make her a very nice "going-away" nightdress in a case, and Uncle said he would feel very honoured if she were to borrow his small leather bag to take it in, and Father gave her sixpence to put in her purse.

Milly-Molly-Mandy felt so excited!

When Saturday morning came Grandpa got the pony-trap ready to go to market as usual, and Milly-Molly-Mandy came skipping down the path, ready to go with him and meet Mrs Hooker as arranged.

Her hat looked just like new, and she had on a pair of nice warm woolly gloves that Grandma had knitted for her, and Aunty's best nice warm woolly scarf, lent for the occasion.

Mother gave her a bunch of late chrysanthemums and a cream cheese for Mrs Hooker, with her love. And then Grandpa got up in the trap and took the reins, and Milly-Molly-Mandy was lifted up beside him. Then off trotted Twinkletoes, and Father and Mother and Grandma and Uncle and Aunty called, "Goodbye, Milly-Molly-Mandy! Have a nice time!" and waved, and Milly-Molly-Mandy waved back till she couldn't see them any longer. And she was really off for her visit!

They didn't see little-friend-Susan or

Billy Blunt as they drove through the village, but Milly-Molly-Mandy waved at their houses, in case they might see her. And then they were out in the open country, and Milly-Molly-Mandy was glad of Aunty's nice warm woolly scarf and her own nice warm woolly gloves.

They came to the town, and got down by the big clock in the market-place, and Mrs Hooker came hurrying up, looking quite different, somehow (for Milly-Molly-Mandy had seen her only once before, and had nearly forgotten what she looked like.)

And then Grandpa kissed Milly-Molly-Mandy goodbye, and went off to do his business in the market. And Milly-Molly-Mandy took Mrs Hooker's hand in its grey kid glove, and went off with her.

Milly-Molly-Mandy had never been away

"Goodbye, Milly-Molly-Mandy! Have a nice time!"

from home to stay before without either Father or Mother or Grandpa or Grandma or Uncle or Aunty, and it felt so strange and exciting.

"Well, Milly-Molly-Mandy," said Mrs Hooker, "I just want to buy some crochet-cotton, and then we will be getting home."

So they went into a big draper's shop, heaps of times bigger than Miss Muggins' shop at home, and Mrs Hooker asked for crochet-cotton. And while she was buying it Milly-Molly-Mandy looked about and felt the purse in her pocket. Presently she saw some pretty little guards to put over the points of knitting-needles, which she thought would be so useful to Grandma.

And suddenly Milly-Molly-Mandy had an idea: What fun it would be to take presents home for everybody! She had five pennies of her own as well as the sixpence Father had given her.

She wondered what everybody would like, and remembered Mother once saying, "Handkerchiefs always make an acceptable present." So when she had bought the guards for Grandma she asked the lady behind the counter if she had some handkerchiefs that weren't at all expensive, and the lady behind the counter brought out a boxful, each one marked with a letter in one corner. So Milly-Molly-Mandy looked at them all, and chose one for Mother with "M" in the corner, and one for Aunty with "A" in the corner. And then she only had two pennies left. She wondered whatever she could get for Father and Grandpa and Uncle with twopence.

Presently Mrs Hooker finished her

purchases, and they went out into the street to go to Mrs Hooker's house. There were such a lot of people, all over the pavement and road, for it was market-day, and there seemed so much to look at that Milly-Molly-Mandy wished she had a dozen pairs of eyes. But still, with only two, she managed to keep one on the shop windows as they passed, hoping to see something which Father and Grandpa and Uncle might like. And suddenly she saw a tray of pink sugar mice in a sweetshop, labelled "Two a penny".

"Oh, Mrs Hooker!" said Milly-Molly-Mandy, "would you mind waiting a moment while I get a sugar mouse to take home to Farver and Grandpa and Uncle?"

So Mrs Hooker held
the leather bag and
chrysanthemums
and cream cheese
until Milly-Molly-
Mandy came out with

a bag of sugar mice in her hand (she had
bought four, and one was to be a goodbye
present for Mrs Hooker). She wished she
could get presents for little-friend-Susan
and Billy Blunt, but that didn't seem
possible, for she had used up all her money.

When they got to Mrs Hooker's house
they put the chrysanthemums in a vase on
the table, and the cream cheese in a dish
on the sideboard. (Mrs Hooker was very
pleased with them.) And then there was just
time before dinner for Milly-Molly-Mandy
to unpack her small leather bag in the little

room she was to sleep in all by herself. And she found Mother had popped in Booby Rabbit, the toy she had won at a party once, and had slept with ever since. She was so glad to see him, and hid him in her nightdress-case so that he shouldn't be seen, because he hadn't been invited. (It was such fun for Booby Rabbit!)

The plates at dinner were so pretty – quite different from the ones they had at home – and so were the wallpaper and the carpet. Altogether, there seemed so much to think about that there wasn't time to say more than "Yes, please," and "No, thank you." But she enjoyed her dinner very much.

After dinner Mrs Hooker said, "I have asked Milly next door to come and spend the afternoon with you, and you can play with my old toys."

Milly-Molly-Mandy was very interested. And then she said, "Will Milly-next-door put her hat and coat on to come here?" – for their nearest neighbours at home were little-friend-Susan and the Moggses, and they lived five minutes' walk down the road (but only three minutes if you ran).

Mrs Hooker said she really couldn't say. And presently the next-door gate squeaked, and then Mrs Hooker's gate squeaked, and then the doorbell rang, and Milly-next-door came in (with a coat on and no hat).

Mrs Hooker told Milly-Molly-Mandy to take Milly-next-door upstairs to her little room, to take her coat off. So Milly-Molly-Mandy played hostess, and let Milly-next-door use her comb, and asked her if her name was really Millicent Margaret Amanda, like Milly-Molly-Mandy's own.

And Milly-next-door said no, it was Mildred.

Then Milly-next-door admired the new nightdress-case lying on the bed, and when Milly-Molly-Mandy showed her the new nightdress inside (which was pink) Milly-next-door admired that too. (She didn't see Booby Rabbit.) But when Milly-Molly-Mandy showed her the handkerchiefs marked "M" for Mother and "A" for Aunty Milly-next-door was quite surprised.

"Oh," said Milly-next-door, "my mother never has her handkerchiefs marked 'M'! She has them marked 'R' because her other name's Rose. What's your mother's other name?"

"It's Polly," said Milly-Molly-Mandy, in a sad little voice.

"Oh, well," said Milly-next-door

comfortingly, "I expect they can use them, even if they aren't quite proper."

But Milly-Molly-Mandy didn't feel very comforted, for she had so wanted to give Mother and Aunty proper presents.

Then they went downstairs and played all the afternoon with Mrs Hooker's funny old-fashioned toys. And when the lamps were lit Mrs Hooker brought out a beautiful paintbox and a fashion paper full of little girls, and Milly-Molly-Mandy and Milly-next-door each painted a little girl very carefully, and cut it out with Mrs Hooker's scissors, and gave it to each other for a keepsake.

And during tea Milly-Molly-Mandy had another good idea: she would paint and cut out some paper dolls, very, very nicely, and take them home to little-friend-Susan for a present! Milly-Molly-Mandy didn't think Billy Blunt would care for paper dolls; she didn't know what she could give him. She wished she had another ha'penny for a sugar mouse.

And now it was time for Milly-next-door to put on her coat again and go home. Milly-Molly-Mandy and she said goodbye, and promised to write to each other and exchange paper dolls.

Milly-Molly-Mandy had never slept all alone before, and when bedtime came she felt quite pleased and excited. Mrs Hooker came and tucked her in, and she admired her new nightdress. Booby Rabbit was under the bedclothes, but he couldn't resist coming up for a peep at Mrs Hooker, and Mrs Hooker saw him and stroked his ears, and said she would certainly have invited him if she had thought he cared to come. And then she kissed Milly-Molly-Mandy goodnight, and Milly-Molly-Mandy lay in the dark and enjoyed going to sleep in a different bed.

Sunday was a nice day. They went to church in the morning, and in the afternoon Milly-Molly-Mandy painted paper dolls for little-friend-Susan.

And then came Monday, and Milly-Molly-Mandy's visit was over. It was in the afternoon that Grandpa and Twinkletoes came with the trap to fetch her home.

She was all ready but for slipping the sugar mouse on to the mantelshelf with a note, "With Love from M.M.M.", where Mrs Hooker would see it when she came in from seeing Milly-Molly-Mandy off; and then Milly-Molly-Mandy was perched in her seat beside Grandpa.

And just as they drove off Mrs Hooker put a little packet of chocolate in Milly-Molly-Mandy's lap, to eat on the way home, and they cried "Goodbye!" to each other, and waved, and soon Twinkletoes' twinkling feet had carried them right out of sight.

Presently Milly-Molly-Mandy, sitting in the trap, had yet another good idea; she could give the little packet of chocolate to Billy Blunt for a present!

So she said, "Grandpa, would you be very disappointed if we didn't eat this chocolate?" adding in a whisper, "I've got something in my bag for you!"

And Grandpa said, "Milly-Molly-Mandy, I'm just feeling too excited to eat any chocolate now!"

So when they got home to the nice white cottage with the thatched roof, and

Milly-Molly-Mandy had hugged Father and Mother and Grandpa and Grandma and Uncle and Aunty, she opened the leather bag, and gave:

Father a sugar mouse – and Father was pleased!

And Mother a handkerchief, marked "M" for Mother. But when Mother saw it she said, "Oh, how nice to have it all ready marked 'M' for Mary!" And Milly-Molly-Mandy suddenly remembered Mother's real name was Mary, and she was only called Polly "for short"! Milly-Molly-Mandy was so relieved that she had to jump up and down several times.

And then she gave Grandpa a sugar mouse – and Grandpa was pleased!

And Grandma the guards for her knitting-needles – and Grandma was pleased!

And Uncle a sugar mouse – and Uncle was pleased!

And Aunty a handkerchief marked "A" for Aunty. But when Aunty saw it she said, "How nice! Mine is marked too – 'A' for Alice!" And Milly-Molly-Mandy suddenly remembered that Aunty and Alice both began with the same letter, and she was so very relieved that she had to jump up and down a great many times.

Next morning she ran down the road to little-friend-Susan's and gave her the painted paper dolls, and little-friend-Susan was pleased!

And later in the day she saw Billy Blunt, and gave him the little packet of chocolate – and Billy Blunt was very surprised, and pleased too, and he made her eat half, and it was the bigger half.

And then Milly-Molly-Mandy wrote a little letter to say "thank you" to Mrs Hooker.

Milly-Molly-Mandy just does enjoy going away visiting!

12 MILLY-MOLLY-MANDY
GETS TO KNOW TEACHER

ONCE UPON A TIME there were changes
at Milly-Molly-Mandy's school. Miss
Sheppard, the headmistress, was going away,
and Miss Edwards, the second teacher, was
to be headmistress in her place, and live in
the teacher's cottage just by the school,
instead of coming in by the bus from the
town each day.

Miss Edwards was very strict, and taught
arithmetic and history and geography, and
wore high collars.

Milly-Molly-Mandy wasn't particularly
interested in the change, though she liked

both Miss Sheppard and
Miss Edwards quite well.
But one afternoon Miss
Edwards gave her a note
to give to her Mother,
and the note was to ask
if Milly-Molly-Mandy's
Mother would be so
very good as to let Miss
Edwards have a bed at
the nice white cottage with the thatched
roof for a night or two until Miss Edwards
got her new little house straight.

Father and Mother and Grandpa and
Grandma and Uncle and Aunty talked it
over during supper, and they thought they
might manage it for a few nights.

Milly-Molly-Mandy was very interested,
and tried to think what it would be like to

have Teacher sitting at supper with them, and going to sleep in the spare room, as well as teaching in school all day. And she couldn't help feeling just a little bit glad that it was only to be for a night or two.

Next day she took a note to school for Teacher from Mother, to say, yes, they would be pleased to. have her. And after school Milly-Molly-Mandy told little-friend-Susan and Billy Blunt about it.

And little-friend-Susan said, "Ooh! Won't you have to behave properly! I'm glad she's not coming to us!"

And Billy Blunt said, "Huh! – Hard lines!"

Milly-Molly-Mandy was quite glad Teacher was only coming to stay for a few nights.

Miss Edwards arrived at the nice white cottage with the thatched roof just before suppertime the following evening.

Milly-Molly-Mandy was looking out for her, and directly she heard the gate click she called Mother and ran and opened the front door wide, so that the hall lamp could shine down the path. And Teacher came in out of the dark, just as Mother hurried from the kitchen to welcome her.

Teacher thanked Mother very much for having her, and said she felt so dusty and untidy because she had been putting up shelves in her new little cottage ever since school was over.

So Mother said, "Come right up to your room, Miss Edwards, and Milly-Molly-Mandy will bring you a jug of hot water. And then I expect you'll be glad of some supper straight away!"

So Milly-Molly-Mandy ran along to the kitchen for a jug of hot water, thinking how funny it was to hear Teacher's familiar voice away from school. She tapped very politely at the half-open door of the spare room (she could see Teacher tidying her hair in front of the dressing-table, by the candlelight), and Teacher smiled at her as she took the steaming jug, and said:

"That's kind of you, Milly-Molly-Mandy! This is just what I want most. What a lovely smell of hot cakes!"

Milly-Molly-Mandy smiled back, though she was quite a bit surprised that Teacher should speak in that pleased, hungry sort of way – it was more the kind of way she, or little-friend-Susan, or Father or Mother or Grandpa or Grandma or Uncle or Aunty, might have spoken.

When Teacher came downstairs to the kitchen they all sat down to supper.

Teacher's place was just opposite Milly-Molly-Mandy's and every time she caught Milly-Molly-Mandy's eye she smiled across at her. And Milly-Molly-Mandy smiled back, and tried to remember to sit up, for she kept on almost expecting Teacher to say, "Head up, Milly-Molly-Mandy! Keep your elbows off the desk!" – but she never did!

They were all a little shy of Teacher, just at first; but soon Father and Mother and Grandpa and Grandma and Uncle and Aunty were talking away, and Teacher was talking too, and laughing. And she looked so different when she was laughing that Milly-Molly-Mandy found it quite difficult to get on with her bread-and-milk before it got cold. Teacher enjoyed the hot cakes, and wanted to know just how Mother made them. She asked a lot of questions, and

Mother said she would teach Teacher how to do it, so that she could make them in her own new little kitchen.

Milly-Molly-Mandy thought how funny it would be for Teacher to start having lessons.

After supper Teacher asked Milly-Molly-Mandy if she could make little sailor-girls, and when Milly-Molly-Mandy said no, Teacher drew a little sailor-girl, with a sailor-collar and sailor-hat and pleated skirt, on a folded piece of paper, and then she cut it out with Aunty's scissors. And when she unfolded the paper there was a whole row of little sailor-girls all holding hands.

Milly-Molly-Mandy did like it. She thought how funny it was that she should have known Teacher all that time and never known she could draw little sailor-girls.

A STRIP OF WHITE PAPER

FOLDED UP FLAT LIKE THIS.

DRAW GIRL, AND CUT OUT,
AND THEN UNFOLD PAPER.

HOW MILLY-MOLLY-MANDY'S TEACHER MADE
LITTLE SAILOR-GIRLS.

Then Mother said, "Now, Milly-Molly-Mandy, it is bedtime." So Milly-Molly-Mandy kissed Father and Mother and Grandpa and Grandma and Uncle and Aunty, and went to shake hands with Teacher. But Teacher said she wanted a kiss too. So they kissed each other in quite a nice friendly way.

But still Milly-Molly-Mandy felt when she went upstairs she must get into bed extra quickly and quietly, because Teacher was in the house.

Next morning Milly-Molly-Mandy and Teacher went to school together. And as soon as they got there Teacher was just her usual self again, and told Milly-Molly-Mandy to sit up, or to get on with her work, as if she had never laughed at supper, or cut out little sailor-girls, or kissed anyone goodnight.

After school Milly-Molly-Mandy showed little-friend-Susan and Billy Blunt the row of little sailor-girls.

And little-friend-Susan opened her eyes and said, "Just fancy Teacher doing that!"

And Billy Blunt folded them up carefully in the creases so that he could see how they were made, and then he grinned and gave them back.

And little-friend-Susan and Billy Blunt didn't feel so very sorry for Milly-Molly-Mandy having Teacher to stay, then.

That evening Teacher came up to the nice white cottage with the thatched roof earlier than she did the day before. And when Milly-Molly-Mandy came into the kitchen from taking a nice meal out to Toby the dog, and giving him a good bedtime romp round the yard, what did she see but Teacher, with one of Mother's big aprons on and her sleeves tucked up, learning how to make apple turnovers for supper! And Mother was saying, "Always mix pastry with a light hand," and Teacher was looking so interested, and didn't seem in the least to know she had a streak of flour down one cheek.

When Teacher saw Milly-Molly-Mandy she said, "Come along, Milly-Molly-Mandy, and have a cooking lesson with me, it's such fun!"

So Milly-Molly-Mandy's Mother gave her a little piece of dough, and she stood by Teacher's side, rolling it out and making it into a ball again; but she was much more interested in watching Teacher being taught. And Teacher did everything she was told, and tried so hard that her cheeks got quite pink.

When the turnovers were all made there was a small piece of dough left on the board, so Teacher shaped it into the most beautiful little bird; and the bird and the turnovers were all popped into the oven, together with Milly-Molly-Mandy's piece (which had been a pig and a cat and a teapot, but ended up a little grey loaf).

What did she see but Teacher learning how to make apple turnovers!

When Father and Mother and Grandpa and Grandma and Uncle and Aunty and Teacher and Milly-Molly-Mandy sat down to supper, Teacher put her finger on her lips to Milly-Molly-Mandy when the apple turnovers came on, so that Milly-Molly-Mandy shouldn't tell who made them until they had been tasted. And Teacher watched anxiously, and presently Mother said, "How do you like these turnovers?" And everybody said they were most delicious, and then Milly-Molly-Mandy couldn't wait any longer, and she called out, "Teacher made them!" and everybody was so surprised.

Milly-Molly-Mandy didn't eat the little grey-brown loaf, because she didn't quite fancy it (Toby the dog did, though), and she felt she couldn't eat the little golden-brown bird, because it really looked too good to be eaten just yet. So she took it to school with her next day, to share with little-friend-Susan and Billy Blunt.

And little-friend-Susan said, "Isn't it pretty? Isn't Teacher clever?"

And Billy Blunt said, "Fancy Teacher playing with dough!"

And little-friend-Susan and Billy Blunt didn't feel at all sorry for Milly-Molly-Mandy having Teacher to stay, then.

The next day was Saturday, and Teacher's furniture had come, and she was busy all day arranging it and getting the curtains and the pictures up. And Milly-Molly-Mandy with little-friend-Susan and Billy Blunt came in the afternoon to help. And they ran up and down stairs, and fetched hammers and nails, and held things, and made themselves very useful indeed.

And at four o'clock Teacher sent Billy Blunt out to get some cakes from Mrs Hubble's shop, while the others laid the table in the pretty little sitting-room. And they had a nice kind of picnic, with Milly-Molly-Mandy and little-friend-Susan sharing a cup, and Billy Blunt having a saucer for a plate, because everything wasn't unpacked yet. And they all laughed and talked, and were as happy as anything.

And when Teacher said it was time to send them all off home Milly-Molly-Mandy was so sorry to think Teacher wasn't coming to sleep in the spare room any more that she wanted to kiss Teacher without being asked. And she actually did it, too. And little-friend-Susan and Billy Blunt didn't look a bit surprised, either.

And after that, somehow, it didn't seem to matter that Teacher was strict in school, for they knew that she was really just a very nice, usual sort of person inside all the time!

13 MILLY-MOLLY-MANDY GOES TO A FÊTE

ONCE UPON A TIME, while Milly-Molly-Mandy was shopping in the village for Mother, she saw a poster on a board outside Mr Blunt's corn-shop. So she stopped to read it, and she found that there was to be a fête held in the playing-field, with sports and competitions for children, and other things for grown-ups. And while she was reading Billy Blunt looked out of the shop door.

Milly-Molly-Mandy said, "Hello, Billy!"

And Billy Blunt grinned and said, "Hello, Milly-Molly-Mandy!" and he came and looked at the poster too.

"When's the fête to be?" said Milly-Molly-Mandy, and Billy Blunt pointed with his toe to the date. And then he pointed to the words, "Hundred-yard races, three-legged races, etc.," and said, "I'm going in for them."

"Are you?" said Milly-Molly-Mandy, and began to be interested. She thought a fête would be quite fun, and decided to ask Mother when she got home if she might go to it too.

A day or two later, as Milly-Molly-Mandy was swinging on the meadow gate after school, she saw someone running along in the middle of the road in a very steady, businesslike fashion. And who should it be but Billy Blunt?

"Hello, Billy! Where're you going?" said Milly-Molly-Mandy.

Billy Blunt slowed up and wiped his forehead, panting. "I'm getting into training," said Billy Blunt, "for the races."

Milly-Molly-Mandy thought that was a very good idea.

"I'm going to do some running every day," said Billy Blunt, "till the fête."

Milly-Molly-Mandy was sure Billy Blunt would win.

And then Billy Blunt asked if Milly-Molly-Mandy could count minutes, because it would be nice to have someone to time his running sometimes. Milly-Molly-Mandy couldn't, because she had never tried. But after that she practised counting minutes with the kitchen clock, till she got to know just about how fast to count sixty so that it was almost exactly a minute.

And the next day Billy Blunt stood right at one end of the meadow, by the nice white cottage with the thatched roof where Milly-Molly-Mandy lived, and Milly-Molly-Mandy stood at the other end. And when Billy Blunt shouted "Go!" and began running, Milly-Molly-Mandy shut her eyes tight so that she wouldn't think of anything else, and began counting steadily. And Billy Blunt reached her side in just over a minute and a half. They did it several times, but Billy Blunt couldn't manage to do it in less time.

After that they tied their ankles together – Billy Blunt's left and Milly-Molly-Mandy's right – with Billy Blunt's scarf, and practised running with three legs across the field. It was such fun, and Milly-Molly-Mandy shouted with laughter sometimes because they just couldn't help falling over. But Billy Blunt was rather solemn, and very keen to do it properly – though even he couldn't keep from letting out a laugh now and then, when they got very entangled.

By the time of the fête Billy Blunt was able to get across the meadow in a little over a minute, and their three-legged running was really quite good, so they were full of hopes for winning some prizes in the sports.

The day of the fête was nice and fine, even if not very warm. But, as Billy Blunt said, it was just as well to have it a bit cool for the sports. As it was Bank Holiday nearly everybody in the village turned up, paying their sixpences at the gate, and admiring the flags, and saying "Hello!" or "How do you do?" to each other.

Milly-Molly-Mandy went with her Father and Mother and Grandpa and Grandma and Uncle and Aunty. And little-friend-Susan was there with her mother, who was also looking after Miss Muggins' niece Jilly, as Miss Muggins didn't care much for fêtes. And Mr Jakes, the Postman, was there with his wife; and Mr Rudge, the blacksmith in his Sunday suit.

There were coconut-shies (Uncle won a coconut), and throwing little hoops (three throws a penny) over things spread out on a table (Mother got a pocket comb, but she tried to get an alarm-clock), and lots of other fun.

And then the Children's Sports began. Milly-Molly-Mandy paid a penny for a try at walking along a very narrow board to reach a red balloon at the other end, but she toppled off before she got it, and everybody laughed. (Miss Muggins' Jilly got a balloon.)

Then they entered for the three-legged race – little-friend-Susan and Miss Muggins' Jilly together, and Milly-Molly-Mandy and Billy Blunt (because they had practised), and a whole row of other boys and girls.

A man tied their ankles, and shouted "Go!" and off they all started, and everybody laughed, and couples kept stumbling and tumbling round, but Milly-Molly-Mandy and Billy Blunt careered steadily along till they reached the winning-post!

Then everybody laughed and clapped like anything, and Billy Blunt pulled the string from round their ankles in a great hurry and cleared off, and Milly-Molly-Mandy had to take his box of chocolates for him, as well as her own.

Off they all started

Then there was the hundred-yards race for boys. There was one rather shabbily dressed boy who had stood looking on at all the games, so Father asked him if he didn't want to join in, and he said he hadn't any money. So Father paid for him to join in the race, and he looked so pleased!

A man shouted "Go!" and off went all the boys in a mass – and how they did run! Milly-Molly-Mandy was so excited that she had to keep jumping up and down. But Billy Blunt presently got a little bit ahead of the others. (Milly-Molly-Mandy held herself tight.)

And then he got a little bit farther – and so did the shabby boy – only not so far as Billy Blunt. And then Billy Blunt saw him out of the corner of his eye as he ran, and then the race was over, and somehow the shabby boy had won. And he got a striped tin of toffee.

And Billy Blunt grinned at the shabby boy, who looked so happy hugging his tin of toffee, and asked him his name, and where he lived, and would he come and practise racing with him in the meadow next Saturday.

The next day, as Milly-Molly-Mandy and Billy Blunt and one or two others were coming home from school, they saw a big man with a suitcase waiting at the crossroads for the bus, which went every hour into the town. And just as the bus came in sight the man's hat blew off away down the road, ever such a distance. The man looked for a moment as if he didn't know what to do; and then he caught sight of them and shouted:

"Hi! – Can any of you youngsters run?"

Milly-Molly-Mandy said, "Billy Blunt can!" And instantly off went Billy Blunt down the road in his best racing style. And just as the bus pulled up at the stopping-place, he picked up the hat and came tearing back with it.

"I should just say you can run!" said the man. "You've saved me an hour's wait for the next bus, and a whole lot of business besides."

"What a good thing you were in training!" said Milly-Molly-Mandy to Billy Blunt, as the bus went off.

"Huh! More sense, that, than just racing," said Billy Blunt, putting his hair straight.

AUTHOR NOTE

JOYCE LANKESTER BRISLEY was born over a hundred years ago, on 6th February 1896. She had two sisters: an elder one, Ethel, and Nina, who was just a year younger than Joyce. The family lived in Bexhill-on-Sea in Sussex, in a house close so the sea that when there was a very high tide the waves would come right into the garden. Joyce's father ran a chemist's shop in the town. Her mother enjoyed drawing and painting, but had to spend most of her time looking after the home and her children.

Joyce and her sisters were all good at art, like their mother, and went to evening classes at Hastings School of Art, taking the train there and back along the coast. By the time they were teenagers, "Eth" (as Ethel was always known in the family) was having her pictures accepted for exhibitions at the Royal Academy in London and was soon selling paintings as a result. Then, through a friend, the girls were invited to meet Miss Brown of the magazine *Home Chat*. They soon began to do illustrations for this magazine, so for the first time all three sisters started to earn money for themselves.

This money was soon to become very important for the family. In 1912, when Joyce was sixteen, her parents separated.

In her diary (writing in French as if to keep it secret) she recorded that her father wanted his family to leave the house. They stayed until Joyce and Nina had finished their term at art school, then the three girls moved with their mother to South London, where Eth had found them a tiny flat.

In London, Joyce and Nina enrolled at the Lambeth School of Art in 1912 – an uncle kindly agreed to pay the fees for both girls. They studied there five days a week for two years. In 1913 they moved to a house with a large room that the three girls could use as a studio.

The outbreak of World War I in 1914 meant that food was scarce. Their mother had to spend a lot of time searching for meat and vegetables she could afford, while the girls worked hard earning money from illustrations for magazines, newspapers and advertisments. Joyce writes in her diary about drawing advertisements for Cherry Blossom boot polish and Mansion floor polish. She also writes about the German bombing raids on London – describing how, in September 1916, the sisters had to get up in the middle of the night and go downstairs for safety, still in their nightclothes and bedtime plaits.

Despite the war, and constant worries about money, family life continued happily throughout this time. In 1917 Joyce records in her diary that Nina (daringly) wants to cut her hair short, and Eth longs to do the same, but Joyce feels "I couldn't – it wouldn't suit me at all". The sisters obviously got along very well together, but nevertheless Joyce wished she had some privacy. She was delighted when, shortly after her twenty-first birthday, she was able to have a room of her own – "My longing, for years and years."

In 1918 they all moved again, to a house with a larger studio. Joyce went with her mother and sisters to the local Christian Science Church. There they met an artist who worked for *The Christian Science Monitor*. As a result, both Joyce and Nina began submitting stories and drawings to the paper, and it was on the Children's Page in October 1925 that the first story about Milly-Molly-Mandy appeared. The idea had come into Joyce's mind one day when "the sun was shining and I longed to be out in the country instead of sitting indoors all day, earning a living . . ."

Milly-Molly-Mandy was an immediate success and soon began to gain a strong following among readers. Joyce records that:

> ". . . boys and girls began writing letters to the paper, to the editors and to Milly-Molly-Mandy herself, wanting to know more about her, asking, Could she come for a holiday by the sea? Could she have a baby sister to take out riding in the pram?

(She couldn't, as she was an 'only' child, but little-friend-Susan could, and did.) Some of the letters enclosed foreign stamps for Billy Blunt's collection (so generous!). One boy wrote all the way from Australia to tell me that 'Father' was shown digging with his wrong foot on the spade (for it seems the left foot is the right foot for digging with!). I wrote back to thank him and promised to alter the drawing before it went into a book – as you may see I did, for it's nice to get things quite correct."

Joyce went on writing stories about Milly-Molly-Mandy for the rest of her life, but she wrote about other characters, too, in books such as *Marigold in Godmother's House* (1934) and *Adventures of Purl and Plain* (1941). She also illustrated stories by other authors and was specially chosen by her publisher, George Harrap, to draw the pictures for the first edition of Ursula Moray Williams' *Adventures of the Little Wooden Horse* (1938).

Joyce always remained close to her sisters. Nina, who became the first and much-loved illustrator of the Chalet School stories by Elinor Brent-Dyer, was the only one to marry. Ethel died in 1961, and some years later Nina and Joyce died within a few months of each other, in 1978.

Joyce Lankester Brisley seems to have been a rather shy person and she obviously didn't like publicity. Once, after two of her pictures had been accepted by the Royal Academy and a journalist wanted to interview her, she telegraphed at once that she "would be out". Maybe she was a bit like Milly-Molly-Mandy herself – happy to be busily getting on with whatever task or errand she'd set herself for the day, and content with whatever good fortune life might bring her.

ADVENTURES OF THE LITTLE WOODEN HORSE

URSULA MORAY WILLIAMS

Dashing, proud and brave – Uncle Peder had never made so fine a horse before.

The little wooden horse loves Uncle Peder like a father and hopes never to leave him. Then the toymaker falls on hard times, and the little wooden horse must go out into the world to seek his fortune. But whether he's working in a coal mine or walking the tightrope in the circus, the loyal little horse has only one thought: to return to his beloved master's side.

Ursula Moray Williams' *Adventures of the Little Wooden Horse* was first published in 1938. Favourite children's author Vivian French, who so loved this story as a child, shares her enthusiasm for this charming little horse in a new foreword. With heart-warming illustrations by award-winning artist Paul Howard, this glorious new edition will introduce a beloved modern classic to today's children.

GOBBOLINO THE WITCH'S CAT

URSULA MORAY WILLIAMS

"I'll be a kitchen cat. I'll sit by the fire and sing like a kettle on the hob."

With his sparky whiskers and magic tricks, no one could mistake Gobbolino for a simple kitchen cat. But that's just what this little witch's kitten longs to be. So, while his sister Sootica learns how to turn mice into toads, Gobbolino sets off to find a family to care for him. Through his many adventures he makes many friends, but he never gives up hope of finding the home he dreams of . . .

The enchanting story of the kind-hearted Gobbolino was first published in 1942. With magical illustrations by award-winning artist Paul Howard and an illuminating foreword by celebrated children's author Joan Aiken, this beautiful new edition brings Gobbolino's story to life for a new generation.

THE MILLY-MOLLY-MANDY STORYBOOK

JOYCE LANKESTER BRISLEY

A little girl with a heart of gold!

This fabulous omnibus edition of twenty-one stories about the ever-popular Milly-Molly-Mandy includes stories from the classic *Milly-Molly-Mandy Stories*, plus ten extra stories taken from later collections – all illustrated with Joyce Lankester Brisley's charming original drawings.

Milly-Molly-Mandy has enchanted generations of readers since the very first stories appeared in *The Christian Science Monitor* in 1925. Her adventures with playmates little-friend-Susan and Billy Blunt remain as fresh and appealing as ever. Young children will love to join Milly-Molly-Mandy as she goes to the seaside, minds a baby, helps to thatch a roof, and goes to a wedding . . .

Perfect for reading aloud, the timeless stories of this cheerful little girl will bring back happy memories for many parents and grandparents, and are a joy to share with children today.

MORE MILLY-MOLLY-MANDY

JOYCE LANKESTER BRISLEY

A little girl with a heart of gold!

This second omnibus edition of twenty stories about Milly-Molly-Mandy is a real treat for all young children. It finds Milly-Molly-Mandy, Billy Blunt and little-friend-Susan having more adventures and even more fun. Joyce Lankester Brisley's original drawings bring Milly-Molly-Mandy's escapades to life as she finds a nest, makes some toffee and goes sledging.

Distinctive in her pink-and-white striped dress, Milly-Molly-Mandy is a little girl with a sweet nature, a happy spirit and an enthusiasm for everything she does. She has found her way into the hearts of readers for over seventy-five years. Sharing this collection with today's children or grandchildren will be like introducing them to an old and very dear friend!

THE BIG MILLY-MOLLY-MANDY STORYBOOK

JOYCE LANKESTER BRISLEY

With new illustrations by Clara Vulliamy

Celebrating over 75 years of Milly-Molly-Mandy!

This special anniversary collection celebrates the enduring spirit of a much-loved classic children's character. Since her creation in 1925, Milly-Molly-Mandy has captivated generations of children. Now she appears in this lavish, full-colour gift edition to enchant today's young readers.

Follow Milly-Molly-Mandy through the seasons, from the joys of helping in the garden in springtime, to singing carols at Christmas. Whether she is running errands, going to the seaside or learning to make pastry, Milly-Molly-Mandy's warm family relationships and her adventures with playmates Billy Blunt and little-friend-Susan are irresistible. The stories are accompanied by Clara Vulliamy's exquisite paintings, which capture Milly-Molly-Mandy's infectious enthusiasm and remain true to the charm and spirit of the original drawings.